Kernowland

Darkness Day

Book Two

To Oliver

Kernowland
Darkness Day

Jack Trelawny

The Chronicles of
ERTHWURLD

CAMPION BOOKS

A catalogue record for this book
is available from the British Library

ISBN 978-1-906815-02-8

Campion Books is an Imprint of Campion Publishing Limited

Illustrations by Louise Hackman-Hexter

Printed and bound in the UK by
Short Run Press Ltd,
Bittern Rd, Sowton Industrial Estate, Exeter, EX2 7LW

First printed in paperback 2013

First published in the UK in hardback 2006 by

CAMPION BOOKS
2 Lea Valley House, Stoney Bridge Drive,
Waltham Abbey, Essex, UK   EN9 3LY

www.jacktrelawny.com

For Tizzie and Louis

Kernowland

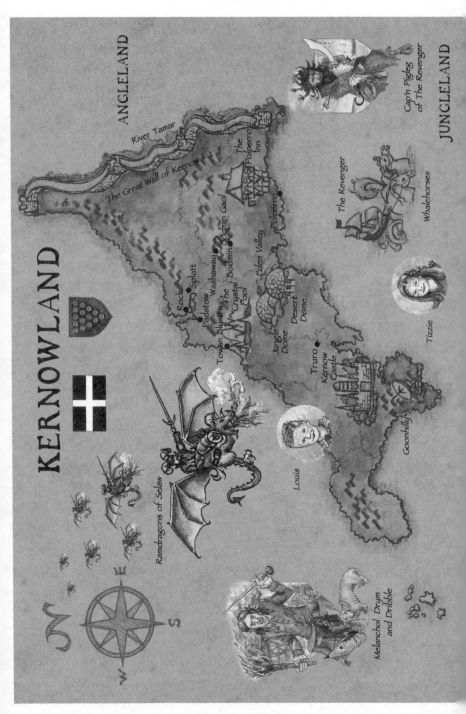

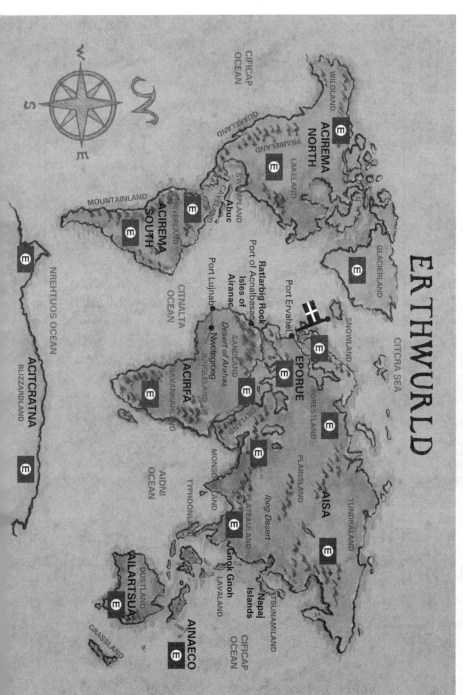

AUTHOR'S  NOTES

Apart from Tizzie & Louis,
the characters and events in this book
are entirely fictitious.

In the *Erthwurld* books,
'Erth' means 'Earth',
and 'Wurld' means 'World'.
Evile is pronounced *ee-vile* to rhyme with mile.
Skotos is pronounced *skoh-toss* – it means 'darkness' in Greek.
Photos is pronounced *foh-toss* – it means 'of light' in Greek.
Graph means 'draw' in Greek, so a *photograph* is…
'a picture drawn with light'.

Websites
There is lots of other information
as well as clickable zooming maps
on the Kernowland and Erthwurld websites

www.kernowland.com
www.erthwurld.com

ONE

Your Brains Are Mine

'Hellllllllllllpp!' screamed a terrified Louis as Monstro's steaming digestive juices blistered his forehead and scalded his nose and cheeks.

'*Your brains are mine!*' gloated the brainboiler.

'*Use the catapult,*' squeaked Misty. '*Aim at the brain.*'

In a few incredibly rapid movements, Louis grabbed his catapult, reached for the ammo belt, fumbled for a cataball, loaded it in the stretchy elastic, aimed, pulled, and fired down at Monstro's brain.

The cataball hit the surface of the boiling, bubbling liquid.

At that very instant, there was a blinding flash of light and a huge explosion.

An unbearable pain seared through Louis' skull as his eardrums burst.

Little Louis knew no more.

TWO

Stinking Buckets

With so many children crammed in to the hold of the ship, the smell was horrendous.

There were only a few toilet buckets to go around and they were full most of the time. One of the younger children had knocked over a stinking bucket during the night. Mr Purgy had opened the hatch to let the bad odours out, but it hadn't helped that much.

Tizzie looked around the hold. There were children from all over Erthwurld whom Pigleg and his crew had collected throughout the previous year as bait for Big Red Grunter.

Some looked as young as four or five. Others may have been fourteen or fifteen. Many were sick from lack of good food and being kept in the hold for so long. Most were in rags. The older children were taking care of the younger ones as best they could.

Although only thirteen, Jack appeared to be the leader. No longer restrained by chains after the Octogon incident, the Red Wizard's apprentice took advantage of the light from the open hatch to introduce Tizzie to some of the other children.

'This is Masai Mara,' informed Jack, pointing to a very tall boy of about fifteen who had shining black skin. 'He's from Savannahland in Acirfa.' Tizzie hid herself partly behind Jack and waved shyly at Masai, thinking that he looked very impressive in his red robes. Masai stared at her for a few moments, then grinned a big grin, showing all his teeth. He said nothing but his eyes were warm and friendly.

'And this is Yin and this is Yang,' said Jack. 'They're

twins from Gnok Gnoh.'

'Hahlo,' said Yang, the boy twin, very loudly, at the same time putting out his hand and shaking Tizzie's up and down very fast. Yin was very much quieter than her brother; she politely bowed her head without saying anything.

'And this little one here is Su Doko,' said Jack, patting a small girl on the head as if he were her big brother. 'She's from the Napaj Islands in Tsunamiland.' Su Doko beamed at Tizzie. She had very intelligent eyes. Tizzie beamed back.

Moving on, Jack then pointed to a girl sitting quietly, cross-legged, in a corner of the hold. The girl had her eyes closed, so Jack didn't disturb her. Tizzie guessed her age at about fourteen.

'She's from Prairieland in Acirema North,' he whispered. 'Her name is Meda. It means "prophetess" in her native language. You'll see why if you talk to her. She can sometimes tell the future.

'And this is Meda's friend, Anpaytoo,' continued Jack, introducing another girl of about twelve. Tizzie learned that her name in her own language meant 'radiant'.

'Hey Jack,' shouted a boy with blond hair and huge biceps. 'Bring ze new girl over here.'

'Meet Hans Berg from the Spla Mountains in Eporue,' said Jack, walking towards the boy and pulling Tizzie by the hand with him as he went.

'Guten Morgen,' greeted Hans, remaining seated. Tizzie knew he was speaking in his own language because she understood that it was German for 'good morning' from lessons at school.

'Not zat it iss ever a good morning on zis stinking pirate ship,' blurted Hans.

'Ssshhhh!' cautioned Jack, looking up warily towards

the open hatch. 'You'll be in trouble if they hear you talking like that.'

'I don't care,' said the rebellious youth, with, it seemed to Tizzie, rather more bravado than was wise. Jack put his hand on Hans' mouth before he could say any more.

'That would be fine if you only had your own safety to worry about. But think of the others; they're relying on us to look after them. After I got lashed, you know we agreed not to upset Pigleg or the crew or do or say anything that might get us into trouble with them, for the sake of the little ones.'

'Okay, sorry,' said Hans, as if he really meant it. 'It's just zat I'm so sick of zis stinking hold. I have to get out of here soon, or I'm going to go crazy.'

'You may not be so keen when we arrive in Jungleland,' warned Jack, his voice lowering to a whisper. 'Masai says this is the height of the feeding season, and the big red boar will be getting hungrier by the day. He'll have widened his hunting grounds to find more food. They'll be finding gnawed bones all over Jungleland by now.'

Tizzie listened with renewed terror at the thought of Big Red Grunter and his pointed tusks and razor teeth.

Unfortunately, a little girl sitting nearby, who was only about five or six, also heard what Jack had whispered.

'I don't want to be eaten bit by bit by that big, horrible, grumpy pig,' she sobbed, as tiny tears trickled down her cheeks.

'There, there, Lucy,' soothed Jack, as he gave her a comforting hug. 'We won't let Grunter eat you, will we Hans?'

'No vay,' promised Hans. 'Vee vill look after you, Lucy.'

At least we've got boys like Hans to protect us, thought Tizzie.

But then, as the big tough youth looked away, she noticed a little tear trickling down his own cheek.

THREE

DOGS! I Hate Them All

Melanchol Drym swiped and slashed the air with Spikey as he strode angrily down the road, ranting and raving like a madman.

'Ungrateful, double-crossing mutt.'

Swipe.

'Treacherous diary-thief.'

Slash.

His dirt-green longcoat flapped as he strode. Passers-by moved to the other side of the road when they saw him coming, to keep out of his way.

A long-haired old dog was sleeping contentedly on the step of a little cottage as Drym marched on.

'DOGS! I hate them all, oh yes I do,' he snarled. 'We'll feed them all to the chewing creatures when "you-know-what" happens Spikey, oh yes we will. Not long to wait now, oh no there isn't.'

Drym went out of his way to walk up the short garden path towards the snoring old dog. Raising Spikey as high as he could, the grey monster bashed the pointed stick down on the sleeping dog's tail.

The dog yelped, jumped to its feet and fled inside to safety.

The old lady who lived in the house had seen what happened through the window. She struggled outside, waving her walking stick and shouting after Drym, who was striding off down the road with a great smirk on his grey face.

'You nasty man; great big bully. If my husband were still here…'

'Shut up, granny windbag,' sneered Drym over his shoulder, with an even bigger smirk that revealed two rows of jagged and rotten brown teeth.

The nasty dustman continued on down the road towards the valley where Wendron lived, still ranting and raving and swiping and slashing Spikey through the air again and again as he went.

'I'm going to get that dog. Oh yes I am.'

FOUR

The Nine Gnomes of Washaway Wood

The journey to Washaway Wood had made Dribble very thirsty. He lapped up the water in the bowl that Plumper had given him.

'Splendid,' said Plumper, when Dribble had finished drinking. 'Now, it's time to introduce you to some of the other gnomes.' With that, he opened the door of his house and waved his arm for Dribble to follow.

'There are nine of us in all. I don't think any of the others will understand your book though, so I think we should wait for Clevercloggs to have first look at it, don't you?'

Dribble nodded his head up and down as fast as he could and barked once as loud as he could to make sure Plumper understood he was trying to say: 'Yes. Definitely.'

'Splendid, that's settled then,' agreed Plumper. The fat gnome picked up the diary and put it under his arm. He immediately wished he hadn't done that. It was still quite soggy from being in Dribble's mouth for so long. Plumper looked around. 'Ah, I know, I've got my handkerchief.' He took a big yellow piece of cloth from his pocket and wrapped it around the diary.

Dribble followed Plumper out of the house and down the winding garden path to the main street of the village. Like many main streets in Kernowland, it was called 'Fore Street'. As he walked beside Plumper, Dribble saw that this street, and all the paths off it, were wiggly and winding. In actual fact, there was not a straight line anywhere in Washaway. All the little houses were

15

higgledy-piggledy, as if they had been thrown together out of bits and pieces. Some of the windows and doors were in very unexpected places. All the gardens were unkempt, and the fences looked as if they had been erected very quickly.

Plumper seemed to guess what Dribble was thinking because he began to explain. 'We gnomes aren't really interested in working or looking after our houses,' he said. 'We like to sit outside – or inside – and talk about adventures and eat sweets and cakes and drink apple juice. We like to play on the swings and seesaws and in the sandpit, or fish in the pool or go for walks; short walks mostly, because long walks are more like work than fun. The rest of us talk about adventures but it's only Clevercloggs who's brave enough to have ever had any.'

Dribble wondered when Clevercloggs would be back. Time was short.

The diary had to be read soon and taken to the King to save Kernowland from the invasion, and the Kernowkids from *Drym's Dungeon* and slavery.

FIVE

Whalehorses

'Get up the ladder and on deck,' shouted Purgy into the hold. 'NOW!'

All the children did as they were told. On deck, Tizzie was glad to be away from the horrid smells, and breathing fresh air again. Some of the older slavechildren were less fortunate. They had been given buckets of seawater and mops, and ordered to slop out the stinking quarters.

'We always clean the ship before coming in to port,' explained Jack. 'We'll soon reach Port Ervahel in Ecnarf; and then the whalehorses will tug us to Jungleland in no time.' Tizzie was itching to ask what a 'whalehorse' was, but felt sure she should know if she was from Erthwurld, so she resisted the temptation.

Port Ervahel soon came over the horizon.

As the ship sailed slowly up the estuary towards the port, Masai Mara, who was tallest, saw them first and pointed.

'There!'

All the children looked. Tizzie couldn't believe her eyes. There were literally hundreds of whale-shaped creatures in the water. But, instead of looking like whales at the front end, the sea creatures all had giant horses' heads and long flowing manes.

As the ship got closer to the docks, she also noticed they each had, not only a whale's tail fin at the back to swim with, but also another tail, like a horse's, above the fin. Each of the horse-like tails must have been ten feet long. These horse tails were all held upright and arched over, so that their tips dangled just a few inches above the water.

The whalehorses were each tethered to their own long wooden landing jetty by a thick rope. Each rope was attached to a large iron ring, embedded in a thick leather collar encircling the forebody of its owner.

'Bet Pigleg only stays long enough to load the provisions and harness up the whalehorses,' said Jack. 'He's dying to get at Big Red. We should be there before the twelfth moon if we start out this afternoon; although I've heard rumours of some stops being planned along the way.'

Tizzie wished Jack hadn't reminded her, once again, about the hungry, razor-toothed pig waiting for them in Jungleland. She couldn't get it out of her mind. She also wondered where they might stop on the way.

Her thoughts were interrupted by lots of shouting and activity amongst the pirates. *The Revenger* was docking and each man had his job to do. In no time at all, the ship was securely tied to the dock with thick ropes.

A gangplank was lowered. Mr Cudgel made his way down the wobbling board, with Purgy bouncing along behind him, panting and nodding and looking up at his master like a loyal pet. The two nasty pirates set off towards the town. Tizzie wondered where they were going.

'Skalliock! Scrump! Get me some whalehorse power!' boomed Pigleg. A couple of his men, who seemed ready and waiting for the order, immediately got into two small boats and started rowing towards the whalehorse jetties.

In no time at all, the men were rowing back towards *The Revenger*, with a thick rope and a pair of reins trailing in the water behind each boat. Tizzie could see that the reins were attached to a bit between the teeth of each whalehorse. The ropes were still tied to the iron rings in their collars.

The great water horses swished their tail-fins up and down as they moved gracefully forward. It was a majestic sight. The giant creatures sang in tandem, as if communicating with each other. The sound was like nothing Tizzie had heard before; a mix between the whinny of a horse and the call of a whale.

As the rowing boats neared the ship, they headed for the bow. Tizzie peered over the edge to take a closer look. The two pirates tied the free ends of the ropes to two thick iron rings, which protruded from the ship, just above the waterline. The leather reins were then drawn up by hooks on the ends of two cords that had been dropped over the bow for the purpose. Another pirate up on deck looped the reins loosely around the bow rail.

Tizzie noticed that the majestic beasts each had letters on their backs.

'Cruel, branding them with their given names, isn't it?' said Jack, who was now beside her. 'Look, can you see? That one is called "Tugger". And the other is "Trailblazer". Probably means one is strong and sturdy, a puller, and the other is faster, a racer. Likely they've been chosen as a good all round team.'

Tugger and Trailblazer turned themselves in the water to face the same way as the ship. Then they slowly swam forwards until the ropes became taut, causing the ship to lurch up in the water at the bow end. Everyone on board was forced to shift their feet to keep their balance.

'Whalemaster, rein those steeds in a while, will ye,' bellowed Pigleg. Following his captain's orders, a tough-looking pirate grabbed a very, very long whip and ran towards the bow of the ship. He took up the reins and jumped into a seat resting on a plank that protruded about six feet away from the deck.

If he slips from the seat, he'll fall in the water, thought Tizzie.

As if he had heard her thought, the man quickly strapped himself securely into the seat with a leather belt and buckle, and then leant well back as he tugged on the reins with all his strength.

'Whoaha, boys. WHOAHA!' he shouted at the top of his voice. This seemed to calm the whalehorses down. They soon settled quietly in the water.

'The bits hurt their mouths unless they do what the whale-master wants,' informed Jack. 'That's how one man can control such huge beasts.'

'Seems like those whale'orses are even keener to get to Big-Red-Pig-Land than I am,' guffawed Pigleg. A few of his men sniggered. The Captain seemed to enjoy his own joke enormously for a brief moment. Then he became serious again.

'As soon as Mr Cudgel and Purgy return from their toilin', we'll be on our way. I want everything ready, lads.'

'Aye, aye, cap'n,' shouted Pigleg's men.

Tizzie reflected for a moment on what she was witnessing. Things here were so different from her own world that it was hard to assimilate them all into her head in such a short time. Erthwurld seemed so cruel and harsh by comparison with her world. She longed for home.

A few moments later, Cudgel and Purgy came into view down in the harbour.

Tizzie's spirits sank even lower at the sight of what they were bringing aboard.

SIX

Clever Cottage

Dribble and Plumper had now reached a very different house to all the others. This one was just as higgledy-piggledy as the rest but the garden was beautiful. It was obviously tended with loving care.

'Splendid, isn't it?' said Plumper. 'Greenfingers lives there and he loves gardening. Flowerpot helps him. We gnomes aren't given a name until our fourth birthday. Then we're called by the one that best suits us.'

The chubby gnome placed his little hands proudly on his big tummy. 'So, I was called Plumper, perhaps for obvious reasons; and Greenfingers was so called because he loved gardening from a very early age. He can make beautiful flowers grow in the middle of winter, you know. Flowerpot loves arranging them to look nice. Everyone knows she loves Greenfingers too. Except Greenfingers himself, of course; he seems more interested in flowers than Flowerpot.'

Dribble was very impressed with the wonderful garden that Greenfingers had made.

As they continued along Fore Street, they soon came to the very last house in the village. It was a little larger than the rest and looked much, much older. There were two long buildings attached to either side of it, which looked as if they had been added a long time after the original house had been built.

'That's Clever Cottage, where Clevercloggs lives. He's got lots of clever gadgets in there. One extension is for his Learning Library, and the other is for his Experimental Laboratory.' Wow, judging by the size of the buildings, Clevercloggs must have a lot of books and do a lot of experiments, thought Dribble.

The path to the house forked three ways in the centre of the garden, with the right fork leading to the library, the left to the laboratory and the central one to the front door of the cottage.

At that very moment, a girnome walked out of the front door of Clever Cottage. She was wearing an apron and carrying a bucket and mop in one hand and a dustpan and brush in the other. Dribble had never actually *seen* a girnome before, although he had heard that they really did exist. Now he knew it was true!

'Ah, Prickle,' said Plumper, 'this is Dribble, and he's brought us a curious book...'

Prickle frowned, looked down at the path and barged past Plumper with a huff before he could finish introducing Dribble.

'She's often like that,' explained Plumper. 'Her job is to stay indoors and do all the cooking and cleaning and washing and ironing for us boy gnomes. That's what girnomes do, you know. I've no idea why she always seems to be in a bad mood; we boy gnomes are such happy fellows.'

Dribble thought he knew why Prickle was in a mood all the time. He would be in a mood too if he had to stay indoors to clean up after everyone, whilst they just sat around and talked or played in the sunshine or the rain or the snow, without taking their turn at the chores. Now it dawned on the little dog why girnomes were so rarely seen... they were always indoors doing the chores.

'Come on,' said Plumper, beckoning Dribble to follow him up the right hand path. There was a sign on the big door that it led to: *Learning Library – Open 24-7.* 'The library may be open all the time,' explained Plumper, as if he thought he was saying something clever and funny and worth hearing, 'but it's only Clevercloggs who ever uses it; the rest of us are too busy eating and drinking and playing.'

Dribble didn't think it was very clever to be eating and drinking and playing *all* the time, when *some* of the time you could be reading books. He was certainly clever enough to know that he couldn't go everywhere and see everything for himself. He had often wished he could read so that he could find out all about the wurld from books.

They entered the library. Dribble looked down the long room. Shelf upon shelf of books stretched from floor to ceiling, all the way to the other end. There must be thousands of them, thought the little dust dog.

'We'll just leave your book here,' said Plumper, placing the sticky diary, still wrapped in his yellow handkerchief, in the top drawer of a big desk at the house-end of the building. Dribble hoped it would be safe there.

'Clevercloggs will love that book of yours,' continued Plumper, as they walked towards the door on their way out. 'He's always solving puzzles and reading about everything.'

Outside, Plumper pointed along a path that wound down towards a large pond, which was surrounded by a glade of trees.

'That's the Playing Place,' he informed Dribble, who could now see that some of the gnomes were playing and talking amongst themselves around the pond.

Plumper set off towards the pond, with Dribble following along behind him.

'Come on, I'll introduce you to some more of my friends.'

SEVEN

Chain Gang

Tizzie watched in despair as Cudgel and Purgy strode triumphantly down the jetty towards the ship.

Behind them followed a chain gang of children in rags, all looking tired, dirty, and frightened. The chains around their ankles jingled and jangled along the harbour cobbles.

'Ah, more bait,' sighed Pigleg out loud, as if well pleased by the sight of so many children in chains.

'All this good news calls for a celebration. Jenny, get me rum and me cheese board and bring it to me cabin. And you can clean up while you're there.'

'Aye, aye, sir, Cap'n Pigleg,' said Jenny.

What a crawler she is, thought Tizzie. She must take lessons in crawling.

'And you, Little Miss Troublemouth,' he barked, pointing his golden hook at Tizzie, 'you can help her.

'And look lively, the both of ya!'

Jenny beckoned Tizzie to follow her. Grudgingly, she did.

They went to the galley and collected the rum, and cheese, and some biscuits, and a board to put them on. His biscuits aren't mouldy like the ones we get, thought Tizzie.

As they carried Pigleg's celebration feast towards the cabin house, Tizzie heard the captain barking orders at one of his men.

'Tell Mr Cudgel I want to see him and Purgy in me cabin immediately. I need to talk to the tattoo.'

EIGHT

The Playing Place

'I can see Fishalot is down there as usual,' said Plumper, as he and Dribble approached the Playing Place.

'Oh, and Seesaw is there too. The other person he's playing with isn't a real person at all. Seesaw has a special stone playmate, called Sawsee, who is exactly the same weight as him and so makes the seesaw go up when he is down and down when he is up. Clevercloggs invented it. Look, he even put a spring underneath Sawsee to make it work.'

That's clever, thought Dribble.

'And the huge oak tree is Old Oaky. He's been around even longer than Clevercloggs.'

Dribble looked at Old Oaky. He had strong branches and large green leaves. A swing was attached to a thick horizontal branch protruding from his trunk. A gnome sat on the swing.

'Hi, Swinger,' waved Plumper.

Swinger waved back. Then, as if showing off for their guest, he began to swing backwards and forwards to an alarming height.

'Longlegs should be about somewhere,' continued Plumper. 'You can't miss him if you see him. He's nearly three feet tall, you know!'

As they walked down the path towards the Playing Place, Dribble was amazed to see a large covered theatre in a clearing, fronted by a magnificent wooden stage.

Plumper explained: 'That's Washaway Theatre, with the Great Stage where we perform our Learning Plays.

Clevercloggs writes them to teach us all about the wurld, since he's the only one who's been anywhere. He says that it's the only way for us to learn if we're not going to read or travel. We can all read a bit of course; we just don't bother very much. The plays are great fun to do. Acting is one of my favourite things, although it's hard to remember the lines. And people come from all around to watch.'

The plum red stage curtains were drawn across the stage. Dribble wondered what was behind them. But, before he could take a look, there was a loud shout.

'On yonder tor!' exclaimed an unusually tall gnome, who had appeared as if from nowhere. He was pointing towards the brow of a hill in the distance.

'Is it them, Longlegs?' questioned Plumper.

'I believe it be they,' answered the tall gnome.

A murmur of excitement spread amongst the gnomes. Dribble looked.

He had very good eyesight and could see something very strange through a gap in the trees.

There, riding along towards them, was a bespectacled old gnome with a very long and bushy white beard.

But he wasn't riding a pony.

Nor was he riding a donkey.

It wasn't a camel either.

Dribble squinted.

It was a green swan!

NINE

Wrinkled Wendron of Coven Cave

Drym arrived at Smog Valley, so named for the permanent murky mist that hung low along its length. The dustman knew the smog was something to do with the industrial scale on which Wendron practiced her witchery. The heavy grey fug gave the whole place a creepy, sinister atmosphere.

Wendron lived right in the depths of the valley, in a converted cave, which had a wooden frontage. There was one small, shuttered window, and a swinging sign above the door: *Coven Cave*.

The shutters of the window were open. Drym stopped outside to listen. He could hear the wrinkled witch debriefing Craw. This was never easy, because the crow couldn't talk.

However, the bird was very clever and could communicate by pointing at the pictures in a special book called, *Craw's Cartoons*. This book had thick pages that the crow could turn himself with his beak. He could also answer, with one squawk for 'yes' and two for 'no', if Wendron asked him a question. Wendron and Craw had made some progress.

'Sohhhhh! A short-legged, long dog took a grey book from Drym to the gnomes?' confirmed Wendron, after Craw had pointed at a series of images in the picture book with his beak.

'Crorrhhh!' squawked Craw enthusiastically, which meant, 'absolutely correct'.

'Well done, my little crorker,' encouraged Wendron,

ruffling the bird's head feathers the wrong way with her long wrinkly fingers, to his obvious discomfort.

Drym began to tremble with the special fear that only his encounters with the wrinkled witch could engender. Before Wendron had retired early to become a full-time witch, she was a school teacher, doing witchery in her spare time. In actual fact, she had been *his* teacher at school.

She still treated all her former pupils as if they were children. And they reacted as if she were still their teacher. Drym, like everyone else, still called her 'Miss Wendron', though much more out of fear than respect.

Miss Wendron had made it her job to be cruel to children all her life, as if getting back at every last one of them for some terrible injury that childkind had collectively caused her. And Drym was certainly no exception; she had made his school life hell.

Although it was a long time since his schooldays, the dustman was still totally petrified of her... and now Craw had told her that Dribble had taken his diary with all the secrets in it. He wondered whether he should go in at all.

As Drym plucked up the courage to enter the cave to confirm the bad news, he saw the familiar sight of Miss Wendron in her teacher's black gown and black mortar board hat, which had a frayed tassel hanging down from it.

No one was quite sure why she still wore the gown and hat. But it was certainly true that she had never been seen out of it since her graduation from teaching college all those years ago.

Out of the corner of his eye, Drym noticed Scratchit, Wendron's mange-ridden cat, observing Spikey suspiciously from her catledge on the wall of the cave. Drym detested cats nearly as much as he despised dogs, and Scratchit knew it well from painful experience. She had often felt the spiteful stab of Spikey.

'I thought you'd come here first,' spat Wendron, as she spun around to face him. Drym could hardly bear to look at her. All the skin on the witch's body, especially her face and hands, was very wrinkly. It was a muddy yellow colour, as if it were a bit rotten and going mouldy. It made him feel sick.

'I'm truly sorry, Miss Wendron, for letting the dog take the diary, oh yes I am,' grovelled Drym, looking around the cave at anything but her skin.

'You will be,' she replied. 'You've been a very bad boy, Drym. Put out your hand.'

Drym's mind travelled back to his schooldays. In a blatant disregard of the ban on corporal punishment for children in Kernowland, Miss Wendron was always calling him out to the front of the class, even if he hadn't done anything wrong. Then she would rap his knuckles with a heavy wooden ruler that she had even given a name: 'Whackit'. This was when he had first become a bully, doing to the younger children what Wendron had done to him.

'Persistent use of whacking' was the reason she had been asked to retire early. Age and festering resentment had not improved the former teacher. Since retiring, she had become even more nasty and bad tempered, and much, much wrinklier. Her hair had gone grey and dry as straw. Her fingers had curled up into claws, and her long nails had become more like talons. The ruler, following some modifications, had long since become her favourite witching wand. But that didn't stop her still using it for whacking.

Back in the present, Drym heard Wendron screaming again.

'I said, put out your hand!'

As always, Drym did as he was told.

Wendron raised Whackit very slowly, as if to maximise Drym's anticipation, before bringing it down as hard as she could across his bony grey knuckles.

'Owwwch!' moaned the dustman through gritted teeth.

'Hahaa! Now, we both feel better for that, don't we young man?' cackled Wendron, in exactly the same way as she had done throughout his schooldays.

'Yes, Miss,' whimpered Drym, before making a feeble attempt to explain himself and get back in Wendron's good books. 'But I just took my afternoon nap for a few minutes and that nasty little, ungrateful little, thieving little…'

'I've got the idea,' interrupted Wendron, raising Whackit again to make sure Drym knew he had to shut up and listen. 'What I want to know is, what was in the diary and how did the mutt know what it said? He wouldn't have taken it unless he knew it was important. He must have overheard you saying something.

'Or can dogs READ these days!?'

Drym feigned innocence, opening out his palms and shrugging his shoulders, whilst pulling a 'who knows' face.

But this didn't fool Wendron for a moment.

'You've been telling secrets to that stupid stick again, haven't you? Didn't I specifically warn you not to do that?!'

Again, Drym didn't answer; but his face showed his guilt.

'I thought so,' hissed Wendron.

'Put. Out. Your. Hand!'

TEN

Clevercloggs and Heavyfeather

Dribble watched as Clevercloggs rode into Washaway to the cheers and waving of his friends. As the wise old gnome and the green swan approached the Playing Place, all the gnomes burst into song.

'Happy birthday to you, happy birthday to you, happy birthday dear Clevercloggs, happy birthday to you.'

The leader of the gnomes beamed and chuckled and wobbled about on the swan's back, in time with the singing.

When he reached the pond bank, Clevercloggs untied two walking sticks that were attached to his saddle and dismounted from the swan's back. Using both walking sticks in one hand for balance, he pulled another very short white stick from his pocket with his other hand.

'Open wide, Heavyfeather, old chap,' he said, as he placed the short white stick in the green swan's beak. The swan gripped one end of the stick tightly, whilst Clevercloggs tugged on the other end. It was extendable and became much longer.

I wonder why he needs that stick, thought Dribble. And why is he called Heavyfeather?

Gong!

A loud gong rang out. The sound seemed to be emanating from behind the plum curtains. The dust dog watched attentively as the curtains began to open, revealing a long table covered in a white cloth.

On the table was more food than Dribble had ever seen in his whole sad and hungry life. There were sausage rolls, and sandwiches, and salads, and cold meats, and jellies, and lots more delicious looking things to eat. A gobbet of drool dripped from Dribble's mouth as he anticipated tasting proper food for the first time ever.

With the aid of his two walking sticks, Clevercloggs began hobbling down the aisle between the theatre seats, heading for the stage. At the same time, the famous explorer gave a strange whistle to the green swan. Dribble thought it must have been some sort of instruction because the bird began moving towards the sound, tapping the ground in front of him with the white stick as he went. Clevercloggs continued to whistle at intervals, as if guiding Heavyfeather with the sound.

Everyone formed a line and took it in turns to grab a plate and take their share of the wonderful banquet buffet. Plumper handed Dribble a big wooden bowl, which the little dog clenched between his teeth as the fat gnome piled all sorts of goodies in to it. Both then left the stage and sat amongst the theatre seats, Plumper on a chair, and Dribble by his side in the aisle.

During the party, Plumper told all his friends about the special book that Dribble had brought with him for Clevercloggs to look at.

After about an hour, and six trips to the buffet table – which was eleven less than Plumper – Dribble was absolutely sure he could not take one more bite of food.

The little dog watched contentedly as Flowerpot, the only other girnome he had ever seen, presented Clevercloggs with his main present.

'It's a silver box with his name on, full of his favourite peppermints,' informed Plumper, who was sitting back in his chair with his hands on his tummy, unable to move because he was so full up.

Clevercloggs, who was clearly enjoying his party enormously, beamed and thanked everybody in a short speech.

As soon as the old gnome finished speaking, there was another loud gong.

Four gnomes went backstage. A moment later, they were proceeding slowly towards the long table, bearing an enormous birthday cake on a huge square board covered in silver paper. Plumper explained there were five hundred candles on the cake, one for each year of Clevercloggs' long life. Dribble thought it looked like a floating bonfire.

'Happy birthday to you...', sang the gnomes again.

Even though he was very full, the little dust dog thought it would be rude to refuse a piece of cake, so he nodded when offered.

After Dribble, and everyone else, had eaten at least three slices of birthday cake, and as the Grand Teafeast was nearing its natural conclusion, Plumper shouted down the table to Clevercloggs.

'Can we show our new friend, Dribble, a Learning Play?'

'Of course we can,' beamed Clevercloggs. 'Which one would you like to see?'

All the gnomes shouted the same thing at the same time.

'*Wendron's Spite!*'

ELEVEN

Tattow the Talking Tattoo

Tizzie was helping Jenny to clean the captain's cabin. Neither of them spoke, which seemed to suit them both; they certainly weren't friends from Tizzie's point of view.

Pigleg entered after a few minutes, apparently quite pleased with everything because he was whistling. Tizzie just looked down and got on quietly with her cleaning, so as not to attract attention to herself.

There was a knock at the door.

'Come in, Mr Cudgel,' barked Pigleg, as he chewed on a large chunk of hard, smelly cheese. Cudgel came through the door first, closely followed by a very apprehensive looking Purgy.

'Well, get on with it,' instructed the captain, with a wave of his hook, 'open yer shirt.'

'Aye, aye, sir,' mumbled Purgy, as he reluctantly unbuttoned his tunic. Tizzie couldn't resist a look. She glanced up. To her amazement, there on Purgy's chest, was the strangest tattoo she had ever seen. It was part face, part skull. Two eyes appeared to be moving from side to side under closed lids. And, if she wasn't very much mistaken, there was a sound coming from it. She listened again. Yes, the tattoo was snoring!

'Wake it up then,' said Pigleg.

Cudgel tapped the tattoo tentatively with his truncheon arm.

'Wakey, wakey, Tattow,' he mumbled, in such a way that made Tizzie want to laugh out loud. But she managed to contain herself.

'Come on, we haven't got all day. I need to know,' shouted Pigleg.

Purgy thumped his own chest with both hands like a gorilla and shouted down at the tattoo.

'Tattow. TATTOW!'

'I'll wake it up,' growled Pigleg, as he rose to his feet and strode purposefully across the room towards Purgy.

Click, thud. Click, thud. Click, thud.

The stout man quivered as Pigleg drew back his hook and brought it down hard on to the sleeping Tattow's nose. There was a dull clunk as Purgy was knocked backwards and fell to the floor, where he lay on his back, winded and gasping for breath.

Click, thud. Click, thud. Click, thud.

Pigleg hurried forward, raised his left knee and stomped his hoof down on Purgy's chest, as he screamed dementedly at the tattoo.

'Wake up, ya lazy skull!'

'Orrrfhh!' puffed Purgy, as even more wind was knocked out of him.

'Err... if I might be so bold Cap'n,' said Mr Cudgel, in an apparent move to protect Purgy from more harm, 'perhaps we could try another way this time.'

'BAH! Whatever does the job,' snorted Pigleg, with a dismissive wave of his hook.

The first mate helped Purgy up from the cabin floor.

'Ready, old friend?' he asked, as he grabbed a fistful of the long wiry hairs on Purgy's chest.

'Ready as I'll ever be,' replied Purgy with a grimace, steadying himself by gripping a rail on the wall behind him with both hands as Mr Cudgel tugged as hard as he could at the chest hair.

'Owwwwwwwwww!' screamed Purgy, as hair was torn

from skin. This did the trick. The tattoo suddenly stirred and opened its eyelids.

Glancing up again, Tizzie noticed its eyes moved independently of one another, and could roll around in different directions at the same time. The tattoo began to move its lips. A very strange voice came out of its mouth.

'Urgh. What. Wossup?! Oh, it's you, Cap'n.'

'Yes, 'tis I, your Cap'n and Master, and don't you forget it. Now tell me what's happenin' in Big-Red-Pig-Land, and you can go back to doin' what you do best... nothin'.'

Tattow closed his eyes again for a few moments.

'My brother reports that Grunter raided a village on the coast last night,' said the talking tattoo. 'He's getting bolder by the day. Took four children in the attack, one of them a citychief's daughter. The Junglelanders are mighty mad.'

'Oh yes, and there's breaking news...' Tattow paused, as if he was experiencing bad reception... 'the Kingchief has just increased the reward to two chests of treasure.'

Tizzie wondered where Tattow was getting his information from. And who or what was his 'brother'?

'Two chests of treasure! Do ye hear that, Mr Cudgel?' gloated Pigleg, his eyes twinkling with greed. The first mate grinned and nodded.

'Aye, Cap'n.'

'Well... what are ye waiting for, ya lubberhead? Let's get this ship on course for Jungleland... and don't spare the whale'orses!' Mr Cudgel didn't need telling twice. He hurried back on deck and began barking orders in every direction.

Back in the cabin, Tizzie was still sweeping.

'Get out of my sight, Troublemouth,' snarled the Captain.

'And you can go too, cabin-girl; all cleaning duties done for today.'

Tizzie went back on deck and sat with the other children.

Soon the ship was ready for the Captain's order to sail.

Pigleg arrived on deck.

Purgy marshalled the slavechildren towards the hold hatch.

Tizzie turned her head to see what was happening.

'Whalemaster, loose those steeds,' boomed the Captain.

The long whalewhip cracked twice and the ship began to move out of Port Ervahel, tugged at surprising speed by the majestic whalehorses.

As the pirate ship sailed towards the open seas once more, Tizzie worried that she was getting further and further away from her little brother.

Oh I do hope you're all right, Louis.

TWELVE

The Long Wooden Box

Mr Sand watched as Louis' stiff little body was put in a long wooden box.

Four soldiers then lifted the box on to a wagon, where the lid was placed on top and nailed securely down.

Mr Sand winced each time the hammer struck.

Lieutenant Liskeard had commandeered the wagon and two horses to transport the box back to Kernow Castle.

Prong was tied to the back of the wagon by his reins.

'Move out, men,' said the young officer, with a wave of his gloved hand above his head.

He then led his troop up the steep slopes of Eden Valley, this time by means of the longer but easier route of winding pathways that would start them on their journey to Kernow Castle.

Mr Sand followed at a distance on Dodger, silently contemplating what he would say to the King.

THIRTEEN

What Drym Wrote

'You wrote what?!' seethed Wendron, raising Whackit to threaten her former pupil once more. Drym put his grey hands to his grey face and cowered against the rocky wall of *Coven Cave*.

'I just wanted to record everything in the diary, oh yes I did,' whimpered the cowardly dustman through his bony grey fingers, 'so that the Emperor would know how clever the ten of us have all been and how well we worked together and how much we helped with Darkness Day and the invasion plans. I thought it might help ensure he'd reward each of us with what we've been promised, oh, yes I did.'

'So, you wrote down the names... of ALL of us!'

'I did, oh yes I did,' agreed Drym, as he dropped his head in shame. For some reason he was still unable to lie to his ex-teacher.

'Fool!' screamed Wendron, raising her wand once more. 'Nobody would have guessed who was involved in the plots and plans until it was too late. Didn't you think what might happen if your words were seen *before* the invasion?'

As she continued to scold him, Drym could see that Wendron was getting crosser and crosser by the second. But, as the raving witch ranted on, he simply couldn't think of one thing to say to save himself.

'If your stupid scribblings get into the wrong hands before Darkness Day, we could all rot in Bodmin Gaol forever. The King's men could be on their way here right now. I can't put spells on them all. And what if they alert the Rainbow Wizards! At least tell me you had the good sense not to write the real names of the Insider and the Young Master in that blasted book.'

Drym smiled pathetically, giving himself away: 'Welllll...'

Seeing in the dustman's manner that he had indeed written the real names of both the Insider and the Young Master in the diary, Wendron exploded.

'That does it! Get out of my sight! I'll recover the book on my own!

'The Young Master will have to know about this. But what am I supposed to tell him? Ehh? That dim Drym, the stupid, disgusting dustman I recommended to be one of the ten, has written our leader's name and all the plots and plans in a book and let it get into the hands of Clevercloggs, the brightest mind in Kernowland and a loyal subject of the King!?'

Again, Drym desperately tried to think of something to say, but could not, as Wendron continued to berate and belittle him.

'I always told you you'd never amount to anything. And now you've proven it... yet again. Well I can tell you one thing, there'll be no slavery franchise for you when the Young Master hears of this. More likely you'll be his first guest in Thunder Tower when he opens it again. Go on, get back to your hovel and await your miserable fate.'

With that, Wendron turned her back on the snivelling dustman and waved him away. Drym went down on his knees, tugging pitifully at the bottom of her black cape.

'No, nohhh. Please, Miss Wendron, please. If we work together and act quickly, we can get the diary back. Oh yes we can. The Young Master need never know. I heard the bird show you that the gnomes have the book, oh yes they have. We can soon get to Washaway Wood if we leave right away, oh yes we can. Just give us one last chance to make amends. Spikey and I will *make* the gnomes tell us where the diary is. Oh yes we will. We can interrogate them. We know how. They'll tell us everything.

'EVERYTHING! Oh yes they will.'

Wendron continued to show Drym her back as she stood, still as stone, as if thinking long and hard about what to do. She finally relented, turning slowly about to stare down at him with her cold, calculating eyes.

'Right then. We'll wait a while to inform the Young Master. But you're going to owe me BIG TIME!'

'Oh yes, Miss Wendron, I will, oh yes I will.'

'You've got one last chance, and you'd better put things right.

'Or you'll have me to answer to.

'And Warleggan! And the Insider! And the Young Master!

'And I wouldn't want to be in your worthless, grey skin if Emperor Evile *ever* finds out that you wrote down the invasion plans! And then LOST them!'

'I didn't lose the diary, Miss Wendron,' protested Drym, 'it was stolen by that...'

'Save your drooling dog-story for someone who wants to listen,' interrupted the angry witch.

'We've got no time to lose. We're no longer safe here. We must leave right away and warn Warleggan that his part in the Darkness Day plot and invasion plans might soon be known to the King. That'll give him some time to decide what he should do.

'Then we'll go to Washaway Wood and interrogate those interfering gnomes.'

Wendron led Drym out through the door of Coven Cave.

'Warleggan's place isn't far by air,' rasped the witch,

as she grabbed up an empty jar from a stock piled against the front wall. 'Just need a little fuel.'

In the large front garden, one corner was clearly designated: *Poison Patch*. A skull and crossbones sign nailed to a post warned of the danger. Another corner contained a very large, rusting hand-pump. Wendron took the jar and put it under the rusty tap.

'Well, don't just stand their, dirt-boy,' she shouted. 'Pump it!'

Drym did as he was bidden, operating the pump by cranking the long arm slowly up and down. Nothing came out at first.

'Keep pumping!' shrieked Wendron.

As he pumped the handle, Drym knew what would eventually emerge from the tap. And, although he'd never actually seen it for himself, he knew it was smelly and toxic. What finally dripped out was a black treacly liquid.

'Ahhh! My lovely Wendroileum,' oozed Wendron, with a level of affection Drym hadn't believed her capable of.

After much pumping, the jar was finally full of the black liquid.

'Follow me,' said Wendron, as she made her way beyond the barbed wire fence that bordered the whole garden.

An array of arched, corrugated iron, mini-hangars, each with double-doors on the front, stretched out into the distance down Smog Valley, as far as the eye could see. The first mini-hangar had a big black 'W' painted on the side. Wendron pointed Whackit at its double-doors and screeched out a spellword.

'Nepo!'

The doors opened, revealing a very strange, black, metal contraption, with folded-up wings.

FOURTEEN

The Skycycle

'Ah, my beautiful Skycycle,' sighed Wendron. 'Not long now, dustman, and the whole Empire will be equipped with my flying machines. And they'll all need to buy Wendroileum from MEEEE! Hahaaa! YES! My pension will be secured! I'll no longer have to live on that miserable pittance I get for all those loyal years of service teaching those ungrateful little brats.'

Drym didn't care about Wendron's pension. His attention was fixed firmly on her infamous flying machine.

'Help me roll it out of the hangar,' instructed the witch. Drym did as he was told.

The Skycycle was a large, modified tricycle with a long back axle that created a very wide wheel-base. This allowed space for two black metal sidecars at the rear, one on each side behind the pilot's seat, which was fixed above a large black fuel tank at the front. A large red 'W' motif was painted on both sides of the tank.

A black pipe dropped down from the bottom of the fuel tank and then curved and snaked along the frame of the Skycycle until it protruded about a foot at the back. The pipe opened up into a funnel, a bit like a trumpet.

Wendron's personal Skycycle had a wicker basket on the front. Drym considered what purpose the basket could possibly serve. Does the wrinkled old hag go shopping like everyone else? he wondered, allowing himself the slightest of smirks at the thought of Wendron at the weekly market.

'What are you smirking at?' quizzed the witch suddenly, without even looking round. Drym had often wondered how, ever since he could remember at school, his teacher knew exactly what he was doing, even if she wasn't looking.

'Come on, come on, we haven't got all day,' chivvied Wendron, as she paced purposefully forward. Dustman followed wrinkled witch towards their intended transport.

Drym now became filled with dread.

He knew the reputation of these contraptions for dropping out of the sky for no apparent reason. The rumour was that Wendroileum was still in its development phase and not really ready to use. But Wendron believed her first formula was the right formula, so no improvements were required.

There *had* been a series of unexplained explosions involving Wendroileum. But no one, except the King, had been brave enough to tell the wrinkled witch to her face that her fuel might be to blame. On the advice of his Sky Safety Council, the King had banned her Skycycles. They were considered 'wholly unreliable and dangerous to public safety at the current stage of development'. The King had, quite fairly in Drym's opinion, said that when Skycycles passed the safety tests, Wendron would be free to sell them in Kernowland.

The story had even made the front page of Kernowland's main newspaper, the *Daily Packet*. It was reported that Wendron had stormed out of the enquiry room after raising her wand to the King. If three of the Rainbow Wizards hadn't been present, anything might have happened.

'I know what you're thinking,' said Wendron, when she saw the look of abject fear on his face. 'But I've never had a problem with any of my craft. It's pilot error every time, that's what it is. And, after Darkness Day, when we've got rid of that stupid King, I'm going to sell my Skycycles all over Erthwurld and make lots of MONEYYYYY! Just you wait and see if I don't.'

Drym kept quiet. Like each of the traitors, he had his own reasons for helping with the Darkness Day plot and invasion plans. But, unlike Wendron, he had nothing in particular against the King.

His issue was that Kernowland did not allow slavery, not of any sort. All the dustman yearned for was the day when slavery would become legal in Kernowland, just like it was in the rest of the Empire. Wendron had promised that the Young Master had promised that the Emperor had promised that he, Melanchol A. Drym, would have the one and *only* slavery franchise in Kernowland after the invasion. One child from every family... the contract was worth a fortune, and it would *all* be his. So, Drym's treachery was 'strictly business'.

'Come on, Disgusting,' sneered Wendron, snapping Drym from his thoughts. Drym got in the seat of the right hand sidecar. It was made of hard, uncomfortable wood. There was no seatbelt. The dustman became even more scared. His legs began to shake.

Wendron unfolded the black metal wings of the Skycycle before putting on her flying goggles and seating herself at the front in the pilot's comfortable padded chair. She then took the cap off the fuel tank and poured in the black, treacly Wendroileum from the jar.

'Crorrhh!'

Craw landed on the crossbar in front of his mistress and closed his claws around it tightly, squawking his approval loudly once more.

'Crorrhh!'

The sly crow could fly on his own, of course, but he

relished the sheer unadulterated thrill of Wendron's unpredictable takeoffs. Anything might happen... and it generally did.

Wendron took a very small bottle from her pocket and prised the little cork from the top.

Pop!

It made a slight popping sound.

Plop!

'Just adding the Sparkit,' she cackled, obviously enjoying herself enormously as she let one drop of the purple liquid drip into the fuel tank. She then replaced the tank cap tightly, securing it with an extra turn.

'Ten seconds and the Sparkit will ignite the Wendroileum... so hold on and brace yourself,' advised the wrinkled old hag, as she gripped the throttle in readiness with her right hand, and stretched out her left hand towards the left grip. The handlebars were so wide that she could only just reach both grips at the same time.

Drym gulped, wondering how on erth he had come to be doing this. He gripped the edges of his seat as tightly as he could with both hands as Wendron counted down.

'Ten, nine, eight, seven, six, five, four, three, two, one…'

Putt, putt… brrrmmmmmm!

A puff of smoke belched from the back of the Skycycle as it burst into life and shook violently, rattling every bone in Drym's body.

'Right, let's get this show off the ground,' screamed the manic witch above the deafening noise, as she taxied to a position suitable for takeoff.

Drym looked ahead. The tall trees at the end of the short runway looked far too close for comfort. The thick smog layer floated mere inches above the tree tops. Drym was even more worried now. Even if we clear the trees, we'll be straight into that filthy stuff!

Seemingly unperturbed by any such concerns, Wendron opened the throttle. A jet of flame roared from the trumpet exhaust behind Drym and they were off, hurtling towards the trees at breakneck speed.

The petrified dustman held on to the sides of his seat for dear life.

Scratchit, in order to avoid a painful stab from Spikey, had waited until the very last moment to run from the cave. She now sprinted along the ground beside them as they sped down the runway. Just as the Skycycle was lifting off the ground, the mangy old feline jumped into the air and landed in the wicker basket.

'Ahhh, there you are,' cackled Wendron. 'Knew you wouldn't want to miss this trip, my little scruffian.

'You can help interrogate the gnomes!'

FIFTEEN

Wendron's Spite

Dribble sat contentedly in the aisle at the front of the theatre, waiting for the Learning Play to begin.

Plumper had been overjoyed to be chosen to play the part of Narrator.

Prickle was not so overjoyed to be playing Wendron the wrinkled witch. She had complained that she had all the clearing up to do after the Teafeast; and there was still that huge pile of ironing. But Plumper had helpfully convinced everyone that she and Flowerpot had all night to do their chores, so Prickle had eventually, after much cajoling, reluctantly agreed to take the part.

Clevercloggs and Heavyfeather were playing themselves.

Dribble became excited as a drum roll accompanied the opening of the curtains.

NARRATOR:
Wendron, the wrinkled witch, had taken a real disliking to Soar, the magnificent swan, the moment she had heard about his perfect looks and his flowing, graceful movements from Scratchit, her hissing, spiteful, vindictive cat.

'Hssssssssssssssss!' hissed all the gnomes as the narrator continued.

For no other reason than pure nastiness, Wendron had travelled a long way on her Skycycle, to Swan Vale, where Soar lived, to cast the Heavyfeather Spellverse on the majestic swan. As you all know, this was a special spellverse she invented to make his feathers so heavy that he couldn't fly.

Soar saw the wrinkled witch coming and, knowing her reputation for spite, fled as fast as his great white wings would take him.

Wendron chased Soar for hours on her Skycycle, before finally cornering the exhausted swan on a bend in a river. As he lay panting and at her mercy on the ground, the witch pointed Whackit, her long rulerwand, and cast the Heavyfeather Spellverse.

WENDRON:
From this time on
The swan won't fly
And all will know
The reason why

Throughout this land
And well beyond
They'll know and fear
My whacking wand

This bird won't soar
In any weather
And all will call him
HEAVYFEATHER!

'Boooooooooh,' booed all the gnomes, almost drowning out Wendron's next spellverse.

And just because
I'm feeling mean
His useless plume
Will be dull green

'Ahhhhhhhhhhh, poor Soar,' sighed all the gnomes.

NARRATOR:
Then Wendron gloated as she added a final nasty stanza to her Heavyfeather Spellverse...

WENDRON:
And one thing more
Has crossed my mind
The former Soar
Will now be BLIND!

'Nooohhhhhhhh, not fair,' cried all the gnomes.

NARRATOR:
With that, the wrinkled witch cackled loudly and flew off on her Skycycle, leaving the newly named Heavyfeather to stumble, sightless, along the riverbank, asking for help from anyone he heard along the way.

But all the passers-by avoided the stumbling blind swan with the strange looking feathers in case whoever had cast the spellverse became cross with them too.

It was then that Clevercloggs the Explorer came floating along the river in his logboat, whistling loudly as always.

As soon as he saw the swan in distress, the wise and kindly old gnome quickly banked his boat to see if he could help.

CLEVERCLOGGS:
Well now, what seems to be the problem here, then?

NARRATOR:
Like the Yellow Wizards, Clevercloggs knew the secret of talking to animals by hearing their thoughts. He listened as the swan telepathically told

of his misfortune.

'My name is S..., S..., Heavyfeather,' began the swan. He had tried to say 'Soar', but he just could not do it; instead he could only say the name the witch had given him.

Heavyfeather went on to explain everything to Clevercloggs, who seemed very kind and understanding.

Clevercloggs immediately knew what to do.

CLEVERCLOGGS:
Now then, it's like this, my friend. You have been unfortunate enough to be the target of Wendron's spite.

I was unfortunate enough to encounter the Triple Trolls some years ago; and they gnawed my legs so badly that they have not been much good for walking ever since.

So, I have bad legs and you can't see. What if the swan were the legs of the gnome, and the gnome were the eyes of the swan? If we work together as a team, we'll both be better off; that's called mutual benefit. We have to make the most of what life sends us, don't you think?

NARRATOR:
Heavyfeather readily agreed, because he could see the sense and logic in the solution.

Clevercloggs made a special saddle, which would be very comfortable for both of them, so that he could ride around on the swan's back. Clevercloggs and Heavyfeather have been working together as a team and helping each other ever since.

THE END

'Hooraaaaaay,' shouted all the gnomes in the audience as they enthusiastically clapped their applause.

'Woof! Woof! Woof!'

Dribble barked loudly. He was having such a good time that he had quite forgotten about the diary and Drym. Then, as the curtain came down on the Washaway Theatre stage, the little dust dog remembered both. He had to get the diary to the King, before the nasty dustman caught up with him.

SIXTEEN

Squire Warleggan of Mound Manor

The Skycycle circled above *The Mound*, a foreboding hilltop on which sat Warleggan's family seat. Wendron appeared to be planning to land the Skycycle *down* the hill. This woman is a menace in the air, thought Drym. Even he knew it was good piloting practice to land *uphill* if at all possible!

Bang! Splutt! Splutt! There was a loud backfire and spluttering from the Skycycle's exhaust. The terrified dustman gripped the sides of his seat once more.

Wendron leant right back in her seat as they came in to land, so that the front of the Skycycle pointed to the clouds. As soon as the back wheels touched down, she pushed the handlebars forward so fast that the front wheel smashed in to the ground.

And then... they were off... bumping and careering down the hill at breakneck speed and completely out of control. Surely she can see the big boulder ahead, thought Drym. But he dare not say anything for fear of another whacking.

Wendron had apparently *not* seen the boulder. This was little wonder, because she had let go of the handlebars with both hands and was trying to catch Scratchit as she was bounced out of the wicker basket high into the air.

The first Wendron knew of the boulder was when it stopped the Skycycle abruptly. The wrinkled old witch was thrown forward, straight over the handlebars, with Drym following shortly after her. Scratchit, never in need of Wendron's assistance, had jumped nimbly clear, and completed a perfect somersault before landing softly on all fours on the grass.

Wendron struggled to her feet. Her matted grey hair had grass and little bits of dry mud in it, and her mortar board hat had been thrown some distance down the hill.

'Get my hat, then!' she screamed at Drym, who reluctantly set off down the hill, not even daring to grumble to himself, in case Miss Wendron heard him. He retrieved the mortar board and climbed slowly back up the hill.

'Come on, dust-boy, come on. We haven't got all day.' Wendron snatched her hat from Drym before brushing it off and placing it back on her head. Then she inspected the damage to the Skycycle. The front wheel was buckled terribly but everything else was still intact.

'Any landing you walk away from is a good landing,' she declared, which Drym thought must surely be a misquotation as he nursed a huge bump on his temple, and pulled up his trouser leg to see the leaking graze on his shin.

They were now quite a way down The Mound. Drym looked up the hill, not relishing the steep climb one bit.

'Well... get in ,' said Wendron. 'We'll taxi up there in no time.'

Drym did as instructed and they snaked slowly up the hill, the buckled front wheel now rattling every one of Drym's bones as they went. How did I ever get mixed up with this woman? he wondered to himself for the thousandth time.

He knew, of course, that now he was in league with her and the other plotters and traitors, it was impossible to go back to the way things were before. But then he consoled himself by thinking about the Kernowland Slaving Franchise that would soon be his.

Not long now, he said in his head. Not long now and all those children will be visiting my dripping dungeon on their way to slavery around the wurld. Oh yes they will.

Wendron and Drym passed through the rusting iron gates of Warleggan's home at the top of The Mound. They were greeted by an eerie sight: Mound Manor.

The old house was a forbidding mansion, with gargoyles looking down on visitors from the roof, and strange statues on the front lawns. A gloomy air pervaded the whole estate.

Warleggan's ancestors had been the local squires for centuries. The present incumbent had let the house get a bit run down. This Squire Warleggan had no interest in spending much of the family fortune on upkeep... his passion was for magic and mutationeering.

They arrived at the huge front doors of Mound House to be greeted by Warleggan in person, his tall frame and weird garb creating a surreal silhouette in the doorway.

'Evening Wendron, Drym,' growled Warleggan in his military manner, 'what a pleasant surprise. All the staff are at my cook's funeral, I'm afraid, so I'm not up to much entertaining. Been taking the opportunity to do a spot of experimenting.'

Not on me, you won't be, thought Drym. He hadn't been relishing meeting Warleggan again so soon after what had happened last time. The warlock had prepared a powder to make Drym's skin a better colour but, during the very first dusting, it had all gone horribly wrong. Drym had been left with an itchy, patchy, red rash all over his grey body for weeks.

'Warlock', in Erthwurld, was the name given to a 'do-it-yourself' magician, an amateur who taught himself at home, rather than learning the art of magic by doing a proper apprenticeship with an experienced wizard. Consequently, in teaching himself by trial and error over the years, Warleggan had made some fairly serious mistakes, especially in his experiments on his own person.

There was no more clear evidence of Warleggan's steep learning curve than his mutilated face, which was covered in warts. He was known, rather unkindly, as, 'the warty warlock', because he had warts all over his body. And the biggest wart was right on the end of his great big bulbous nose. Drym hated having to look at Warleggan, even more than he hated looking at Wendron. But, how ever much he tried not to, Drym always found himself staring at the nose-wart, wondering why the warlock didn't pluck at least *some* of the long, thick, black hairs that grew out of it.

Drym also knew, from his sifting of the Kernowland rubbish, that, in keeping with his family military tradition, Warleggan had applied to join the Kernish Army as an officer. But, for the first time ever, a Warleggan had been refused a commission.

'Far too violent for the army; possibly criminally insane,' the psychological profile had said. On hearing of the rejection, the mad squire had broken in to the barracks and stolen the profile. He had ranted and raved at Mound House for hours before screwing it up and throwing it away. From that moment on, he vowed that he would one day avenge himself on the Kernowland military.

Warleggan looked even stranger than he had done last time. The warty warlock was wearing his protective outfit; an attempt to shield himself from his own spells, powders, potions, and other magical experiments that may or may not go wrong.

The outfit made him look very weird. From bottom to top, it consisted of long boots that came right up his legs, a bit like fisherman's waders, which were worn over his camouflage trousers. Drym knew that the boots were made of a material the warlock had invented himself, a cross between rubber and plastic.

An old family breastplate, from a suit of armour used by his ancestors in ancient battles, was worn over a camouflage jacket, whilst a dented tin miner's hat, complete with candle-holder and flickering permacandle, crowned the whole ensemble.

A pair of long, thick, fireproof gloves, attached to either end of a frayed piece of cord, was hanging around his neck, so that the gloves dangled and danced around as he moved.

'We're not here on a social visit, I'm afraid,' complained Wendron. 'Drym here has something to tell you.' Despite the introduction, it was Wendron who explained to Warleggan what had transpired, with Drym filling in the gaps when he was told to.

When he heard that *Drym's Diary* had been stolen by Dribble and probably taken to Clevercloggs, the wise old gnome, Warleggan agreed it was no longer safe to remain at home.

'We've no time to lose. I'll come with you to get the diary.'

Wendron nodded her approval. Warleggan was a man of action; she liked that about him. Although his ability as a magician was certainly suspect, the squire was her kind of man. Nasty, vicious, extremely well armed, and totally without conscience or remorse, he was the perfect partner for the dark work they had to do. He was the only person she allowed to call her 'Wendron'.

'I'll get my Warcoat,' said Warleggan.

As they got to the door, the unkempt warlock walked up to a coat stand on which was hanging a long, camouflage-coloured coat, with lots and lots of pockets sewn all over it.

'We'll see how the gnomes like some warlock warfare,' growled the belligerent squire, as he swiped up his Warcoat from its hook and marched purposefully out of the door.

SEVENTEEN

The Armoury & The Evstika

The dustman, the witch, and the warlock strode along a path that took them through a wooded area of the Warleggan estate. They soon came upon a clearing, which had what looked like the entrance to a fortified cave in the middle. The entrance was painted with various hues of camouflage green and surrounded with barbed razorwire. There was a sign fixed along its top edge:

KEEP OUT

MOUND MANOR ARMOURY BUNKER
INTRUDERS WILL BE SHOT

Warleggan unpadlocked the dark green doors. The trio descended down a few steps, which led to an underground corridor. So this is the Armoury Bunker, thought Drym, amazed at the scale on which the fortification had been constructed.

At the end of the corridor were two swinging doors, which Warleggan kicked open with his boot. Inside, the first thing Drym saw was a huge red flagbanner draped along the back wall. A thick black 'E' was displayed within a white circle in the centre of the flagbanner.

'Ahhh, the Evstika,' sighed Wendron, 'the sign of the future. Not long now and Evile will rule Kernowland...

and all ten of us will prosper like never before.' I won't, if I don't get that diary back, thought Drym. Double-crossing mutt! I'm going to make him wish he'd never been born. Oh yes I am.

The dustman watched as Warleggan approached a huge cagetank made of thick glass. Inside were dozens of writhing, wriggling ropes.

'Snake-eyed slitherropes,' he declared proudly, as his two cronies watched the ropes slithering around like snakes inside the cagetank.

'My latest mutation. Part snake and part hemp rope. With a living snake's eye at each end. All I have to do is say the spellverse and they're entranced into action. They give chase, seek out and tie a slip knot around any prey I tell them to, and then drag the victim back to me for dealing with.'

Drym now remembered Warleggan's keen interest in mutationeering. He was a bit of an amateur at that too. His mutants occasionally turned on him without warning. The scars were all over his body; another reason for the protective clothing.

Warleggan put on one of his thick fireproof gloves, which covered his hand and half his forearm. Drym wondered why the warlock needed the gloves, since the slitherropes had neither teeth nor claws. Are they going to burst into flames? As if hearing Drym's thought, Warleggan spoke aloud.

'They can give you a nasty rope burn if they slipknot you when you're not expecting it.' Safely gloved up, the warlock took the top off the cagetank.

Hisssssssssssssssssssssssss.

'Hear that?' preened Warleggan. 'Put the hiss in as an afterthought. Nice touch, eh?'

'Splendid,' agreed Wendron, as the warlock reached in, grabbed up a handful of at least twenty writhing slitherropes, stretched a pocket, and stuffed them in it. Drym was amazed to see that they all fitted in to the small pocket. A few of the ropes immediately tried to escape their new confines. But, as they poked their eyes out of the pocket, Warleggan shoved them roughly in again and zipped it up.

'Right, we'll also need stenchshells,' he said with relish, at the same time selecting four egg boxes and filling them with what looked to Drym like ordinary eggs. Once again, Drym was amazed to see all four boxes fit in to one of the Warcoat's pockets.

'Make sure you don't break one by accident,' warned Warleggan proudly. 'The stench I've created can incapacitate an enemy for minutes at a time.' Drym made a mental note not to break a stenchshell by accident.

'And let's take some heat-seeking stunstones as well,' added the warlock, who was clearly becoming very excited at the prospect of attacking the gnomes. 'Throw them in the general direction of your target and they seek out any warm-blooded thing running away from you and stunnify it for a whole minute! Ideal for a capture raid, where your objective is to hold and interrogate, rather than to kill.'

'Like them. Take plenty,' instructed Wendron.

Into a pocket went the stunstones.

'And something special for that dog you're after,' said Warleggan, looking straight at Drym with his wild eyes. 'A snarebolas! Twirl it above the head like this, aim... and release.' The three iron balls and ropes of the snarebolas flew across the room and wrapped around the legs of a stuffed animal, snapping a shin bone with a crack in the process.

'Magnificent! Oh yes it is,' exclaimed Drym, as

Warleggan retrieved the weapon. He began to think that Warleggan wasn't such a bad fellow after all.

Into a pocket went the snarebolas.

'We'll need these as well,' said the warlock, winking at Wendron as he picked up three red armbands, which had the same white circle and black 'E' as the flagbanner emblazoned on them. '*General Warleggan.* Got a bit of a ring to it, don't you think?'

'Yes, I'll say,' agreed Wendron admiringly. 'You'll be able to wear that Evstika with pride when you start your new job on Darkness Day. Not long now.

'What about your Skyscooter?' queried the wrinkled witch. 'We may need it. I've got the fuel.' Drym could see from Warleggan's face that even he, the normally fearless warlock, was wary of using the Skyscooter that Wendron had built for him.

'Well, Wendron... old dear... you see, it's like this... well, um... I'm not sure it's working at the moment.'

'Just bring it, man; if it doesn't work I'll fix it in the field.' Like most men who had any experience of dealing with her, Warleggan didn't relish an argument with Wendron. It was much easier to just do what she wanted. So, giving a quick nod to register his compliance with the witch's suggestion, Warleggan paced over to a contraption made of black metal, which was resting against the wall of the armoury.

Very similar to a child's scooter propelled with the foot, but man-size, it comprised a flat board with a little wheel at either end. A small pair of handlebars, set at waist height, was connected to the board by a pole. A clip-on fuel tank was attached to the pole and an exhaust pipe arrangement, a bit like that of the Skycycle but a lot smaller, ran down the pole, along the board and funnelled out at the back.

Warleggan grabbed up the Skyscooter and removed the detachable pole, fuel tank, and pipe. Drym watched in amazement as the warlock then proceeded to put the whole dissembled collection into a pocket. The Skyscooter board, pole, and pipe were far too long to go in the pocket, and yet they disappeared straight into it. Likewise, the fuel tank was too wide to fit in, but the pocket simply stretched to accommodate it and then shrank back to normal size once it was in.

Drym wondered what else was contained in those pockets. They covered every available inch of the Warcoat.

'I'll just lock up,' said Warleggan, before putting three huge padlocks on the doors of the armoury and setting two booby traps designed to blow up any burglars.

'Must remember I've set them this time,' he mumbled to himself under his breath.

On reaching their transport, Drym and Warleggan jumped into the sidecars of the Skycycle; Warleggan behind Wendron to the left, and Drym to the right.

Wendron added the Sparkit to the Wendroileum, grabbed the wide handlebars, and waited for the ignition.

Bang! Brrrrmmmm!

They rattled down the hill until gaining enough speed to take off again. The climb was smooth enough and they levelled out high above Kernowland.

As they flew along, the wrinkled witch and the warty warlock began an animated discussion about exactly how they were going to interrogate the gnomes. Drym thought about getting back the diary and how he was going to kill Dribble with Spikey's help.

EIGHTEEN

The Diary Code

After they had all enjoyed the Learning Play, Clevercloggs hobbled away from the Playing Place on his walking sticks, with Dribble, Plumper, and Heavyfeather accompanying him.

Plumper took the opportunity to ask Clevercloggs if he could look at the book Dribble had brought with him. To Dribble's delight, they went straight to the Learning Library to retrieve the diary.

In the library, Clevercloggs picked up the grey book from the drawer, unwrapped it from Plumper's yellow handkerchief, and began flicking through the pages.

'Oh dear, some of the pages are stuck together,' he complained. 'I'm afraid that makes the task somewhat more difficult.'

Then they went next door to Clever Cottage, where Clevercloggs made himself comfortable in his favourite armchair. First, the brainy gnome turned to yesterday's page to see the last thing that Drym had written in the diary.

'What strange language is this?' he mused, scratching his chin in the way that he often did when deep in thought. 'Oh yes, I see, it's all in code.' After just a few moments, he appeared to have made sense of something.

'Oh my, oh my. Oh my, my, my,' said the wise old gnome, as if he were very concerned by what he was reading. Plumper couldn't wait a moment longer: 'Well, what does it say?'

'Yesterday's entry begins with: "Jowbtjpo. Ebsloftt

Ebz",' answered Clevercloggs.

'Yes, but what does that *mean*?' sighed Plumper, exasperated by the suspense of it all.

'To decode a code properly, it's best to write it down,' informed Clevercloggs, as he rummaged in a draw for some graph paper. He began writing as Plumper and Dribble watched, the plump gnome having lifted the little dust dog on to a suitable chair so he could see the table top.

'Now, we just have to substitute the previous letter of the alphabet for the letters in the code, like this...'

J	O	W	B	T	J	P	O.	
I	*N*	*V*	*A*					
E	B	S	L	O	F	T	T	
E	B	Z						

Whrrrrrrrrrrrrrrrrrrrrrrrrrrrrrrrrrrrr.

At that moment, before Clevercloggs could decipher the code any further, they heard a strange whirring sound outside.

Then there were louder noises.

Bang! Crash! Boom!

Then screams of terror.

'Aaaahhhhhhhhhhhhhhhhhhhhhhhhh!'

NINETEEN

Air Raid Over Washaway Wood

Hearing the commotion outside, Plumper hurried over to the window of Clever Cottage. He saw his friends fleeing in every direction. They were screaming and pointing to the sky.

Looking up, Plumper could see Wendron circling overhead, as if readying the spluttering Skycycle for a landing.

Warleggan dropped stenchshells from his sidecar. They only had to smash near their target to do their evil work. Below, Greenfingers and Flowerpot were caught unawares in the garden as two stenchshells smashed on the new decking they had just finished adorning with pot plants. The gardener and his number one fan collapsed as the awful odours overcame them.

Drym, meanwhile, excited and energised by the fear of his intended victims, forgot his own fear of flying and stood up in his sidecar. He snarled and waved Spikey in his left hand like a man possessed, shouting and swearing as he rained down stun-stone after stunstone on the scattering gnomes with his right.

Below, Fishalot, oblivious to everything going on around him as usual, had been quietly fishing by the pond. He knew nothing about the stunstone that made a direct hit on his head and stunnified him instantly. Seesaw was hit as he dived from his seewaw. Swinger had seen the stones drop from the sky on to Fishalot and Seesaw. He jumped off his swing, falling over in the process. Clambering to his tiny feet, he ran, screaming in terror, trying desperately to reach the cover of the trees in the Playing Place. A stunstone missed him by inches. Luckily, it was a faulty one, and it wedged in the ground behind him as he fled. Miraculously, he made it to the trees.

Plumper had been momentarily petrified by what he saw. Clevercloggs had now hobbled to the window to see for himself.

'It's Miss Wendron... and she's got Drym and Warleggan with her.'

And Spikey, thought Dribble. A shiver of fear went along the little dog's spine. Dribble knew it would be his very last beating if Drym and the sharp stick ever caught up with him.

'We must get the diary to the King,' warned Clevercloggs. 'If it says what I think it does, we've no time to lose. The future of Kernowland is in our hands.'

With that, Clevercloggs opened a secret panel on his desk and pulled a tiny lever inside it. A small sliding door in the floor started to open, revealing stone steps leading underground.

As the door was opening, Clevercloggs grabbed his big rucksack and gathered up all sorts of gadgets and gizmos, very quickly throwing them in before giving further instructions.

'Dribble, Heavyfeather, you come with me down this tunnel.

'Plumper, you'll never get through the tunnel door... HIDE!'

Where can I hide? worried Plumper, a quiver of fear going through his whole body. However, despite his urge to find a hiding place, his inquisitiveness got the better of him, and he couldn't resist watching all that was going on outside through the window of Clever Cottage.

The stenchbombs and stunstones had done their deadly work. Seesaw lay stunnified on the grass. Greenfingers and Flowerpot lay stenchified on the decking. Fishalot sat stunnified by the pond.

The Skycycle came in to land on Fore Street as the other gnomes scattered in all directions. Swinger ran for the ploughed fields. Prickle ran for the far woods. Longlegs ran for the high hills.

Wendron kangaroo-hopped down the street. When she finally did manage to land, the buckled front wheel caused the Skycycle to bump and wobble and veer sharply off to the right, where it came to a halt in a prickly hedge.

The wrinkled witch, warty warlock, and dreadful dustman were all entangled in the hedge. Plumper giggled to himself, thinking that they looked quite comical. But he soon remembered that these attackers from the sky brought menace and danger to the gnomes of Washaway Wood.

Warleggan managed to extricate himself from the hedge first.

'Armed combat,' he declared loudly, 'this is what I was born for!' As he stepped from the wreck, the warlock's Warcoat became snagged on a thorn. He pulled at it roughly. Rip! The coat tore as the insane squire strode purposefully away, clasping a fistful of writhing slitherropes in his outstretched hand.

What are they? worried Plumper, as he watched the ropes wriggling furiously in their master's grasp.

Wendron and Drym were soon striding along behind Warleggan.

'Loose the ropes then,' shouted the wrinkled witch, whose grey matted hair now had little bits of hedge in it. 'Hurry! Before they get too far away, man.' Warleggan dropped the slitherropes to the ground, at the same time chanting his spellverse.

Seek all gnomes
Who try to flee
And bring them home
To warty old me

Wendron couldn't believe her ears. She knew Warleggan was very bad at magic in general and spellverses in particular, and only about half of what he tried ever worked at all, let alone well. But that spellverse was absolutely terrible, even by his amateur standards. It was quite possibly the worst she had ever heard.

However, to her complete bafflement, the spellverse seemed to work. The mass of ropes spread out and slithered off at high speed in pursuit of the fleeing gnomes.

Plumper watched in despair. Swinger, who was no athlete, was caught before he got across the first field. Two slitherropes encircled each of his feet and began dragging him back towards the village.

Two more ropes followed Prickle in to the far woods. A few moments later she was dragged out of the trees by her ankles.

Longlegs was fastest and managed to get furthest away in the shortest time. As the tallest gnome reached the nearest hill, he began to run up it. The slitherropes slithered after him, chasing him up the slope. Half-way up the hill, Longlegs began to tire. Three slitherropes caught up with him at the same time. They wrapped around his ankles and began pulling him down the hill. He shouted and waved his arms all the way back to Washaway.

The slitherropes were now dragging the seven captured gnomes back from all directions, one by little one, to the waiting inquisitors, who had taken up a position underneath Old Oaky.

Fishalot, still stunnified, was sitting up in his fishing position, clasping his fishing rod in both hands as he was dragged along on his bottom. Prickle's skirts were being pulled up over her waist, exposing her petticoats and bloomers as she was dragged along.

'Oh really, really, this is too, too much,' she was

complaining in her best moaning voice.

Plumper was full of thoughts about what he could do to help his friends, which meant that he still hadn't taken the advice to hide. Unbeknownst to the brave little fellow, whilst he had been witnessing the cruel capture of the other gnomes, two slitherropes had made their way towards Clever Cottage through the long grass. One had already arrived at the back door.

The other slithered up a drainpipe, along the gutter, then up the slope of the thatched roof. It paused to peer in through the skylight, seeking sight of its prey with its snake-like eye.

Plumper heard something drop on to the table behind him. He turned.

The slitherrope reared up like a cobra poised to strike.

Plumper recoiled in shock and fear, momentarily petrified.

Regaining his senses, the plump little gnome started to waddle for the back door. He managed to lift the latch and get one leg out. The rope outside the back door slip-knotted his ankle. The other rope slithered across the room, encircled his other ankle and tied itself securely around it. Plumper was sure he heard the slitherropes hiss triumphantly as they both tightened their grip.

The rough ropes burned the skin on his ankles as they began dragging him along the ground on his back. He was dragged around to the front of the house and through the cabbage patch in Greenfingers' garden.

As he was bumped and bounced along the ground, Plumper managed to raise his head just high enough to see where he was going. He was heading straight towards the three triumphant tormentors.

The dustman, the witch, and the warlock awaited him with crazed expressions on their faces.

A wave of abject fear washed over him.

TWENTY

Upsify Them!

The three tormentors glared down at the eight gnomes.

'Upsify them!' yelled Drym, as he swiped Spikey back and forth in his enthusiasm for the impending inquisition. Upsifixion was a terrible practice that was administered all over Evile's Empire. It involved hanging some poor unfortunate upside down from a tree or post by ropes tied around their ankles. The captive gnomes quivered at the mere thought of it.

'No! No! Please,' they cried, as Warleggan pointed his warped wand and cast his spellverse.

To begin our diary enquiry
All gnomes with slitherropes tied
On this big green tree
Should now be upsified

Urgh! That really is an awful spellverse, shuddered Wendron to herself. It was so bad that she was embarrassed on Warleggan's behalf.

Unfortunately for the gnomes, the often inept warty warlock was having a good day. The slitherropes immediately did his bidding. They snaked around the tree trunk, dragging each of the screaming gnomes up it in turn, like a helter-skelter in reverse.

When the ropes reached Swinger's swingbranch, they slithered along it at incredible speed. The gnomes were left dangling upside-down in mid-air, with Plumper at one end of the line nearest the trunk and Swinger at the other end, nearest his swing.

As the gnomes were upsified, their little red hats fell off, one by one, and were left lying on the ground in a row underneath them.

'You can't do this, it's illegal in Kernowland,' moaned Prickle. 'You'll be in trouble if we tell.'

'It soon will be legal, oh yes it will,' sneered Drym.

'Shut up, Dusty,' barked Wendron, making it patently obvious to everyone that she was in charge. 'It's time for The Register. Get on with it!'

Drym mumbled grudgingly under his breath as he walked along the hanging line of upsified gnomes. He hated the fact that Wendron was humiliating him in front of them. Of course, he was too scared to say anything to her, so, like all bullies, he was going to make himself feel better by taking it out on those weaker than himself. The bully's mood improved visibly as he relished the task in hand.

'Right then, it's time to tell uncle Drym who's here today.'

The gnomes' names were stitched in big letters on the front of their garments. Even though they were upside-down, Drym could read the names perfectly well. But it would be much more fun to make them say their names aloud.

The nasty dustman went along the line, poking each gnome in the ribs in turn with Spikey.

'Name!' Poke.

'Ouch! Swinger.'

'Name!' Poke.

'Ouch! Prickle.'

'Name!' Poke.

'Ouch! Greenfingers.'

'Name!' Poke.

'Ouch! Flowerpot.'

'Name!' Poke.

'Ouch! Fishalot.'

'Name!' Poke.

'Ouch! Seesaw.'

'Name!' Poke.

'Ouch! Longlegs.'

'Name!' Poke.

'Ouch! Plumper.'

'Only eight?' queried Wendron, for the first time, in all the excitement, realising that Clevercloggs wasn't there. 'Where's the swotty one?'

There was silence along the line.

'You may think you're being brave,' snarled Drym. 'But, before this night is out, you're going to tell us everything, oh yes you are.

'EVERYTHING!'

TWENTY-ONE

Tickle Prickle

Plumper had been upsified for what seemed like ages. All the blood was running to his head.

'Where's Clevercloggs?' screamed Wendron.

'And has a drooling dog been here with a grey book?' added Drym, pointing Spikey along the line and snarling to show them it was going to be very bad news for gnomes if they didn't tell.

They all felt the stab of Spikey, over and over again.

No one told.

Wendron joined in, smacking them on the legs with Whackit.

No one told.

Apparently somewhat surprised by the resistance of the gnomes, and just a little tired, the three inquisitors walked away a few paces and formed a huddle.

Plumper could just hear what was being said.

'Can't Spikey just kill one?' pleaded Drym. 'That'll make them talk.'

'Or make them clam up even more,' said Warleggan.

'Yes, no killing yet,' decided Wendron.

Plumper was very proud of the other gnomes. Even though they all knew that Dribble had brought the diary to Clevercloggs, none of them had told anything. He took the opportunity of the brief respite to whisper something along the line.

'The longer we can hold out, the better chance Clevercloggs and Dribble have got. Pass it on.'

The trio of inquisitors returned from their discussion, just as the last gnome had got the message from Plumper.

The next torture, catlicking, was administered by Scratchit on Wendron's instructions. The mangy old cat moved amongst them as their heads dangled a few inches off the ground, licking their faces with her sandpaper tongue. Urghhhhhh, thought Plumper when it came to his turn, her breath smells of fish and garlic.

Despite the horrible catlicking, no one told.

Warleggan and Drym, getting crosser by the second, removed the gnomes' shoes and their long red socks. All the socks had darns and patches. Their removal revealed only seventy-nine wriggling pink toes; Greenfingers had lost the little one from his right foot in a nasty accident with a sharp spade.

Now it was time for 'crowclaws'.

'Claw them Craw,' cackled Wendron, who was enjoying herself immensely. Craw did as instructed, flying from his perch on the swingbranch to land on the gnomes' little feet, where he dug his claws deep in to their sensitive soles.

'Owwwchhhh!' screamed each of the gnomes when it was their turn.

Despite the pain of the crowclaws, no one told.

Drym then prodded them all over again with Spikey, this time much harder.

Still none was telling.

The sun was rising in the east. The gnomes had now held out all night and Plumper was beginning to hope that their tormentors might give up. It was then that Wendron switched tactics.

'You're all being very, very stupid,' she told the array of upsified gnomes hanging from the branch before her.

We've been quite nice so far. But time is getting short, and you leave us no choice.'

The gnomes shivered at the thought of what was coming next.

'Who will be first, I wonder,' continued Wendron, as she scanned her wild eyes along the line. Although they were all friends, the gnomes could be forgiven for hoping that, whatever it was Wendron was going to do to them now, it wouldn't be them to go first.

The wrinkled witch made her choice.

'That one,' she said, pointing as she spoke.

'Tickle Prickle.'

'Ohhhhh nohhhhh,' gasped the gnomes as one.

This was a good plan on Wendron's part. She had just remembered a little known, but in this instance, important, fact. Gnomes can't stand being tickled. This was especially true of girnomes.

Prickle screamed and screamed as Warleggan, Drym, Scratchit, and Craw mercilessly tickled her all over.

Scratchit tickled her ears.

Craw tickled her toes.

Drym tickled her tummy.

And Warleggan tickled her neck.

Plumper could just about bear Prickle's torment.

But when she wet her knickers... he knew it was time to put a stop to all this.

He shouted above the noise of Prickle's screams.

'I'll tell.'

TWENTY-TWO

Jowbtjpo. Ebsloftt Ebz.

Plumper knew that, if he told, the dustman, the witch, and the warlock would find out that Clevercloggs, Heavyfeather, and Dribble had escaped with the diary and were on their way to Kernow Castle to warn the King.

But he had no other choice. He didn't really get on with Prickle that well, because she was cross with him all the time, but he couldn't just let her be tortured by such horrible tickling.

Who would be next? Flowerpot? Plumper couldn't bear the thought of little Flowerpot being tickled so mercilessly. She might never get over it. Grudgingly, the plump little gnome reached inside his pocket.

'Here,' he said, handing over the graph paper on which Clevercloggs had begun deciphering the diary.

'Ha! I knew it, oh yes I did,' said Drym triumphantly. 'That clever gnome *has* seen the diary... so the dog *must* have been here.'

'Give me that', rasped Wendron, grabbing the graph paper from Drym's grasp.

Plumper watched and listened carefully. He saw the wrinkles on Wendron's face quiver in anger as she scanned the letters that Clevercloggs had written.

J	O	W	B	T	J	P	O.	
I	*N*	*V*	*A*					
E	B	S	L	O	F	T	T	
E	B	Z						

'CALL THAT A *CODE*!' she screamed at Drym, who recoiled in horror at what was on the paper.

'Give me a pencil,' ordered the witch. Drym fumbled around in his coat. Of all the times to have forgotten his pencil, this wasn't the best.

'Sorry, Miss Wendron, don't seem to have one on me, oh no I don't.'

'Useless... good-for-nothing... dirtbag!' she stuttered, hardly able to find the words to express her rage.

Warleggan, showing no emotion, took a charcoal writing stick from one of his pockets. It was the pocket with the writing paper and rubbers and paperclips and all sorts of other useful stationery in it. The squire handed the charcoal over.

Wendron looked at him, her frown turning to a slightly wonky smile as she was reminded of another reason why she liked Warleggan a lot; he always had what he needed in one of his pockets.

Charcoal writing stick in hand, the wrinkled witch took a few seconds to finish deciphering the code.

J	O	W	B	T	J	P	O.	
I	N	V	A	S	I	O	N	
E	B	S	L	O	F	T	T	
D	A	R	K	N	E	S	S	
E	B	Z						
D	A	Y						

'There, *INVASION*!!! *DARKNESS DAY*!!!' she shrieked, waving the sheet of paper in Drym's face. 'Some secret code, that is.'

'But, Miss Wendron, little ears...' cautioned Drym, moving his eyes in the direction of the eight, upside-down gnomes, who appeared to be listening intently to all that was being said.

'Fat lot of good trying to keep it a secret now,' complained the witch. 'The brainy gnome has the diary... and he'll soon decipher your childish code. That blasted book will be well on its way to the castle by now, and the King will soon know everything too.'

'But we could intercept the gnome before he gets there, oh yes we could,' petitioned Drym hopefully. 'They can't be there yet, oh no they can't.'

'Yes, thank you, Disgusting,' moaned Wendron. 'I had thought of that one. But, as you well know, there are two roads to Truro and we have no idea which one he'll take. If we choose the wrong one, we'll miss him.'

'We could split up, oh, yes we could,' suggested Drym. 'There's always the Skyscooter.'

'Now there's a good idea, for once,' admitted Wendron, grudgingly. 'Warleggan, we'll take the main road, and you take the back road. That way, we'll surely catch the gnome before he gets to the King.'

'And the dog,' added Drym, immediately wishing he hadn't.

'Will you shut up about that stupid dog!' screamed Wendron.

'What shall we do with the squirts?' asked Warleggan, whilst nodding in the direction of the upsified gnomes all dangling from the tree.

'They're no use to us now,' rasped Wendron, with a look that showed her evil intention.

'Torch the tree!'

TWENTY-THREE

Sparksticks

The eight upsified gnomes began to tremble as they realised that their tormentors were going to set fire to Old Oaky... with them still hanging from the swingbranch. They wriggled and squirmed but it was no use. The slitherropes were tightly bound around their ankles and they were securely tied to the tree.

Plumper watched Warleggan reach into a pocket and bring out a thin piece of wood about the same size and shape as a lolly stick. It had what seemed to be a sandpaper coating at one end.

'Ahh, Sparksticks,' smirked Wendron. 'Amongst my very favourite things, you naughty old warlock, you.'

Warleggan grinned back, whilst scraping the sandpaper end of the stick against one of his long fingernails, at the same time uttering a spellverse.

Sparkstick strike
And light your fire
Of oak and gnomes
Make a pyre

'Good spellverse,' praised Wendron, as the sparkstick burst into roaring flames at the sandpaper end. Warleggan had been careful to hold the other end but he was revelling in Wendron's praise so long that the fire burned down the stick and singed his fingers.

'Owwch!' he cried, dropping the flaming Sparkstick

onto the grass, where it continued to burn ferociously. Wendron looked to the heavens in despair.

'Under control,' declared Warleggan, soon regaining his composure. The warlock pulled a padded fire-glove from one of his pockets, then held it up for Wendron and Drym to see.

'Carry them everywhere,' he said. 'Come in handy all the time.' Quickly putting the fire-glove on, Warleggan picked up the Sparkstick and threw it vertically up into the air, whereupon, it flew off towards the tree.

'Hahahaaa!'

Wendron cackled, and Drym smirked, as the flames first took hold at the base of the tree, and then began to roar upwards. Old Oaky swayed his upper branches from side to side, as if he could feel the heat of the fire. As a grey, choking smoke began to engulf them, the gnomes squirmed and wriggled even more, desperately trying to free themselves.

'Now, let's go and find ourselves the last of the gnomes,' said Wendron, as she made her way towards the Skycycle.

'And the double-crossing, drooling dog!' mumbled Drym under his breath.

Wendron and Drym removed the Skycycle from the hedge. Warleggan liberated the Skyscooter from its pocket, and Wendron filled the small fuel tank with Wendroileum.

The Skyscooter set off at low level, with Warleggan wobbling about on it as he tried to maintain control. The Skycycle was soon in the air once more. As she levelled off, Wendron looked back at the plume of thick, grey wood-smoke rising into the air above Washaway Wood. She cackled spitefully.

'That'll teach the little interferers to mess with Miss Wendron!'

TWENTY-FOUR

Frozen Solid

Louis opened his eyes inside the long wooden box. Thin shafts of light streamed in through little holes in the lid. He couldn't move a muscle, not even his mouth to shout for help.

He began to panic. Where am I?

Just then, he heard the squeak of nails being pulled from wood and the lid of the box was removed. He squinted to shut out the brightness, which initially hurt his eyes.

A moment later, a familiar friendly face peered in, blocking some of the light. Mr Sand's lips moved. Louis could only hear a faint whisper and he quickly realised there was something wrong with his ears.

'Ah, splendid, you're thawing at last,' sighed Mr Sand with delight. 'We may even have you out of there before we get to the castle. I know you can't speak and you certainly won't hear too well. Just blink once if you can understand me.'

Louis blinked. He could just about hear what Mr Sand was saying. 'You fired the blue cataball to save yourself from Monstro. Blue is the catafreezing ammo. Unfortunately you were a little too close to the icy explosion and, although thrown clear, *you* were catafrozen too. It's a wonder you weren't more seriously injured.'

Louis wondered if catafreezing was different from normal freezing, as Mr Sand continued.

'The ointment on your face is for the blistering. And we've put special pads on your ears, which contain little tiny healing organisms. They're mending your eardrums a little bit at a time. Your hearing will soon be back to normal. And we put you in this box, with special warming glow-plants all around you, to thaw you out as quickly as possible. It doesn't do to be catafrozen too long. Any more than two days and you might never wake up.'

This was a lot of information for Louis to take in. He strained his eyes to the sides and could just see the golden glow of the plants that surrounded him.

'The lid keeps all the warmth in,' explained Mr Sand. 'We had to nail it down to stop it falling off on the bumpy road. You're a lucky young man, I'd say. You could have been killed. Monstro has boiled much bigger brains than yours, I can tell you.

'All the men think you're a princely hero of course, what with holing Scurvy's mug at a hundred paces and then coming out on top in a tussle with the biggest and nastiest brainboiler in the wurld!

'Actually,' he continued with a wink, '*I* think you're something of a hero too!'

The ice around Louis' mouth had now thawed just enough for him to manage the faintest smile for the kindly Mr Sand.

'I've rolled your Kernow Catapult and Kaski in your cape. Here, I'll put them in the box by your side. Now, we'll just put the lid back on for a bit more thawing, and we'll have you well again in no time.'

Louis strained to give his friend a bigger smile as the lid was lowered.

It was then that he remembered another friend.

What had happened to Misty?

TWENTY-FIVE

Meow

Meow, the Eden cat, toyed with the frozen blue mouse, rolling it from side to side with her paws, all the while wondering why it had a key stuck in its mouth. She picked the mouse up in her teeth and walked behind the domes, along one of the service paths that she knew so well.

The cat soon arrived at a steaming heap of rotting vegetation, marked with a sign which read: *Kernow Castle Compost*. Meow leapt on top of the heap and dropped the frozen mouse from her mouth. That should warm it through a bit, she thought.

Then she went off to work.

* * *

Misty hadn't felt a thing when he landed on the compost heap. He was thawing out gradually but, so far, the only part of himself that he could move was his right eyelid. Unfortunately there was nothing wrong with his sense of smell. He didn't like being in the rotting rubbish one little bit.

Misty was almost sure the cat had gone away. The brave little mouse knew he had to risk having a look. He opened his eye, just a little bit, and took a look around to assess the situation. He was right; the cat had gone.

Misty hoped the thaw would take as long as possible. He felt sure that, as soon as he was soft enough to eat, he'd be cat food.

How on Erth could he escape?

* * *

Meanwhile, Meow had started work. Many of the Kernowfolk visited Eden Valley to see the plants from all over the wurld. It was Meow's job to rub up against their legs and mew hungrily when they were dining in the *Indigo Eating Place*. More often than not, people would throw bits of food down on the floor for her to eat. She called it, 'working the crowd', and, today, she was doing especially well.

'Ahhh, look at that sweet tubby tabby,' said an old lady to her husband, before stroking Meow's tan fur and dropping a chunk of pasty meat on the floor for her to eat.

The cat mewed and rubbed up against the old lady's leg again. Another chunk of pasty meat fell to the floor. Easy pickings from the mugs today, thought the cat.

Meow was very fat and lazy, possibly due to her rather sedentary occupation coupled with an excessive intake of food. Normally she wouldn't dream of bothering to catch mice; that was far too much like hard work. But mouse meat was one of her favourite dishes. It hadn't been on her menu for as long as she could remember. And that frozen mouse-meal had landed right next to her when she was walking along the path near the Carnivore Cage. It hadn't even needed chasing!

When it landed on the path, she had immediately decided it would be great for dessert, but only when it was a bit less crunchy.

The cat was relishing the prospect of eating the mouse.

Ice-mouse, she thought, as she put on her false purr and rubbed gingerly up against another visitor's leg... scrumptious!

TWENTY-SIX

Knowledge Is Survival

The Revenger sailed along at high speed as it was pulled through the water by the whalehorses. Ever since they had set out from Kernowland, Jack had organised the older children to give regular lessons as best they could, so that the younger children, who were missing school, could learn all about Erthwurld.

Jack had explained to Tizzie his reason for organising the lessons: 'To make sure that as many children as possible know as much as possible about Erthwurld. The more they know, the more likely they are to be able to survive when we escape.

'Knowledge is strength, knowledge is survival.'

With this in mind, Tizzie listened as attentively as she could to all the lessons. Neither Jack nor anyone else knew it, but she had more to learn than any of them about this strange new place.

The lesson was being given by an older girl called Pritti Gud, whom Tizzie had heard was from an exotic land in the east, called Aidni. With no pencil or paper available in the hold, Pritti was using scraps of cloth that had been torn into the rough shapes of the continents to help her give the lesson.

'There are seven continents in Erthwurld. In alphabetical order, they are: Acirfa, Acitcratna, Acirema North, Acirema South, Ailartsua, Aisa and Eporue.'

'What about Ainaeco?' piped Polly Honolulu.

'Well, I'm not sure if all those islands make up a continent,' pondered Pritti, as if trying to consider her answer very carefully.

'My father said that all the islands put together do make a continent,' complained Polly indignantly. 'It's just that most of it is underwater, and the islands are really the tops of mountains.'

'Well, actually, I don't know if that's right,' said Pritti, 'but for now we can include it as a continent until we can ask someone who knows more about it. So, we'll say there are eight continents, and Polly's people live on the continent of Ainaeco.'

'Which people live on the others?' asked Lucy, who was always full of questions.

Pritti did her best to answer: 'People now live on every continent but this wasn't always true. There was originally only one tribe of human beings, the Blackskins of Acirfa, who called themselves, the First People. Over thousands of years, this tribe spread out all over Acirfa, before exploring new lands and migrating to every other continent of Erthwurld.

'They encountered very different lands and climates to what they were used to, and, over thousands more years, their skin colour and other characteristics changed to suit each new environment. Over a long period of time, the one tribe of Acirfa became the five tribes of Erthwurld.

'Who can tell me what the five tribes are?'

'The tribes are the Blackskins, Brownskins, Redskins, Whiteskins and Yellowskins,' said Su Doku.

'Very good, as usual, Su,' praised Pritti.

In the light of what she had just learned, Tizzie looked around her as the lesson continued. She could now see that the children in the hold were a cross-section of all five tribes of Erthwurld. Some of them looked like they might even be a mix of two tribes.

'Right you lot, on deck now,' growled Purgy, down through the hatch. 'And make sure four of you stay to do the bucket rota!'

TWENTY-SEVEN

Three Cheers For Prince Louis

Louis awoke with a jolt as the lid was removed from the box once more. His ears seemed to be much better. He could clearly hear the sound of stomping boots. As the young boy sat up, he found himself looking straight at the soldiers, all marching along in time behind the wagon.

Mr Sand, who was riding alongside on Dodger, climbed aboard the wagon.

'You've been in a long sleep, young man,' he began, 'and, I must say, you seem to be extremely durable. The toughest men in Erthwurld would take a couple of days to thaw, but you've shown incredible powers of recovery. It's rather remarkable.'

Louis now found he had also recovered his voice a little: 'Yes, I feel quite good,' he croaked.

'Well I'm very glad you do,' continued Mr Sand, with a smile. 'I certainly wasn't looking forward to presenting your frozen self to the King and having to ask for help, from Dr Looe and Nurse Tudy, in thawing you out and repairing your ears.'

Mr Sand then untied the bandages covering Louis' ears.

'Better get you back on your mount. Take it steady though. You should remember you're still suffering from catafreezia.'

'OK, I will,' agreed Louis. 'Here, Prong,' shouted the young prince to his Tor pony, who was still tethered by a long rope to the back of the wagon.

'*Fantastic!*' he heard Prong exclaim in his head, '*my Prince is well again.*'

With that, the silver steed galloped towards the rolling wagon.

In a few rapid movements, Louis leapt to his feet, undid the tether knot of the rope and jumped high into the air before landing in the saddle on Prong's back. Mr Sand rolled his eyes to the sky in disbelief. They had just agreed Louis would take things steady.

The soldiers showed their approval of the young royal warrior, as if they were proud that he was a cousin of their King.

'Three cheers for Prince Louis,' shouted one.

'Hip, hip, hoorah!

'Hip, hip, hoorah!

'Hip, hip, hoorah!'

Far from telling his men to be quiet, as expected, Sergeant Stout smiled at Louis and actually joined in the cheering.

Louis puffed out his chest a little and waved one arm in the air as he lapped up the applause.

But, as he brought his arm back down, his ebullient mood quickly faded.

How could he be happy for a moment whilst his sister was still a prisoner of the pirates?

TWENTY-EIGHT

Dark Clouds On The Horizon

The slave children on board *The Revenger* were on another of their deck breaks, so that the hold could be cleaned yet again. With so many young children in the hold, this had become an all too regular occurrence. It had been another bad night for filling and spilling toilet buckets.

Tizzie was getting used to some of the hardships now, but everything was so new and different in this terrible place that she was still very concerned that she might give herself away.

As the ship sailed south, it had been getting hotter and hotter by the hour.

'I'd love to go swimming in the sea,' sighed Polly Honolulu. That sounds good, thought Tizzie, as she mopped the sweat from her brow.

'Not a good plan,' advised Juan Espanya, an older boy with dark hair and brown eyes. 'The sea from here to Acirfa is infested with piranhasharks.'

'What are they?' asked little Lucy.

'Sea hunters,' answered Juan. 'Part piranha, part shark. They hunt in shoalpacks of up to a thousand mouths. Each mouth has a hundred zigzag teeth. A shoalpack is like one big Chewing Creature. It can smell prey in the water from five kiloms, and de-flesh it in seconds. And it can smell blood from even further away; ten kiloms or more. Believe me, little one, you don't want to go swimming in *that* water.'

After hearing this, Tizzie definitely didn't fancy a swim either.

It was then that she heard the foreboding rumble in the distance.

'Look! Thunderbolt clouds.' Jack was the first to see the grey-black masses in the sky as they came over the horizon. Lightning flashed and zigzagged around within them.

'Weather weapons,' informed Jack, speaking to some of the younger children who were watching in awe. 'Created artificially at sea by mutationeers on a weather-warship. Normally used in the early stages of an invasion. As soon as it is overhead the target on land, a cannon on the ship fires an igniterball into the cloud. This sets the weapon off. Lightning strikes everywhere below until the weapon is spent or the enemy can destroy it. Very unpredictable. If the wind changes, it might even come back out to sea at you.'

'Look! Vulturerats!' shouted Yang, pointing to the air. 'A whole squadron.'

'Carrion scavengers,' explained Jack. 'They'll eat anything. Ideal for a quick clean up after a battle. Long pink tails, two rodent legs at the front, two bird legs at the back.'

'There! Bird carriers,' shouted Juan, pointing to the sea.

Squint, the new pirate lookout, had also seen ahead.

'Cap'n! Empire forces on the bow! Ten dozen vulturerats. Two dozen carrier ships.'

'Evasive action, men,' boomed Pigleg. 'All hands on deck. Whalemaster, get those whale'orses turning. Full ahead starboard... and get them slaves below!'

The children were hurriedly marshalled into the hold by Purgy. As they sat in the semi-darkness, they considered the situation.

'Thunderbolt clouds can only mean one thing,' worried Jack, addressing his remark mainly to his older companions. 'Evile's waging war.'

'Do you zink he's fighting ze rebels?' asked Hans, as if he hoped that would be the case. 'They are strong in Ecnarf.'

'Maybe,' said Jack. 'Meda, can you tell us where they're heading?'

The Redskin girl nodded sagely before closing her eyes. 'I will try.'

As the others looked on anxiously, the young prophetess began softly chanting in her own language. After only a few moments, she frowned seriously and opened her eyes.

'What do the ancestors say,' asked Anpaytoo expectantly. 'Where are the invaders heading?'

Meda looked troubled as she answered.

'Kernowland.'

Tizzie's heart sank as she heard this. Louis might still be there. If there was a war, he might come to harm.

'But it can't be Kernowland,' said Jack. 'We have the Rainbow Wizards and the Forcesphere and all the other defences. Evile has never been strong enough to invade.'

Tizzie was momentarily happier at this news... until Meda spoke again.

'Something has changed,' she whispered.

'I sense treachery.'

TWENTY-NINE

The Famous Forcesphere

As he rode Prong over the brow of a big hill, Louis' eyes opened wider and wider in wonderment at the sight that greeted him. From his high vantage point, he had a good view. There before him stood Truro City, which was composed almost entirely of round houses. They were arranged in concentric rings, with a series of ring roads dividing them.

Kernow Castle stood on another hill in the centre of the city, surrounded first by a moat and then by the innermost ring of houses. The castle had been built in the shape of a perfect circle. With its thick outer wall, imposing battlements, and twelve spire towers set at equal intervals along an inner circular wall, the stronghold looked more magnificent than any of the castles Louis had ever seen in his picture books.

A huge, cylindrical, dome-topped tower, positioned in the exact centre of the castle, rose cloudwards. It was much taller and wider than any of the spire towers, which formed the points of a clock around it. Twelve corridors spread out from the central dome tower, like spokes on a wheel, each connecting with one of the twelve spire towers.

The dome roof had been constructed as two halves. They were peeled back and the dome was open in the middle, like an observatory in operation. A dazzling column of white light beamed vertically into the sky through the opening. Louis followed the beam with his gaze until he had to look away because its brilliance hurt his eyes. An array of rainbows stretched over the castle and the town. Louis was fascinated by them.

'It hasn't been raining, Mr Sand,' he said inquisitively, 'why are there rainbows everywhere?'

'Ah, that's the Forcesphere being tested,' came the answer. 'We test it once a day at exactly three o'clock. The sun reflects off the surface of the Forcesphere and makes rainbows.'

Louis was none the wiser. Mr Sand apparently supposed this because he explained further: 'Godolphin the Great created an invisible, defensive sphere, a forcefield of light, in the shape of a ball, a bit like a bubble. It was designed to protect all the people of Kernowland against an invasion. This bubble is the reason why Kernowland is the only free place left on Erth. It has become famous throughout Erthwurld as a symbol of Kernowland's stand against the tyranny of Evile and his evil Empire.'

'How big is the forcefield?' asked Louis, trying to imagine how such a thing could work.

'When it is at full power, the sphere can expand to a diameter of three kiloms, so that it protects the whole of the city. In the event of an attack, all of the people of Kernowland would be protected by the bubble, as long as they could make it to the boundaries of Truro. Most of the Forcesphere is above the ground, guarding us from attack by air or ground forces. But some of the sphere penetrates the erth right underneath the castle, to guard against subterranean attack.'

'But who would be able...,' began Louis.

'I'll explain more later,' said his mentor, as they passed the ring of houses that formed the outer limits of the city.

'For now, I should teach you something about the Trurofolk; you're bound to meet some of them at the Banquet Ball tonight.'

THIRTY

Tea-time in Truro

Kernow Castle loomed ever larger as Louis rode Prong through the outer limits of Truro towards the centre of the city. Looking around him, he noticed that each round house had a cone-shaped thatched roof with smoke rising from its point.

'It's tea-time,' whispered a beaming Mr Sand. 'Warm scones straight from the oven... with jam and cream!'

Louis smiled back. The Bennetts had enjoyed a cream tea on their last holiday. Remembering his family made him feel sad. Then Mr Sand spoke again and brought him back to the moment.

'The Kernowfolk have long believed that, to stay healthy, they need to eat six meals a day, every day,' confided the little man, rather earnestly. Louis thought Mr Sand might be joking, but he seemed very serious as he continued.

'We all learn, from a very early age, that to go without any meal, just once, could lead to all sorts of health problems. Our mothers make sure we have breakfast, brunch, lunch, afternoon tea, dinner and, just before bed, a nice bit of supper to settle the stomach and help the sleep.'

'What do people eat?' asked Louis, with genuine concern, as he tried to imagine what it would be like having to force down six meals a day. He could barely eat the food that his mum gave him three times a day, let alone twice as much.

'Well, they like to start with a hearty Kernish breakfast,' began Mr Sand, 'to set them up for the day. At dawn, they might have a bowl of porridge, followed by kippers, then bacon, eggs, hog's pudding, mushrooms, tomatoes, and baked beans, normally with four or five slices of toast. Mid-morning it would, likely as not, be three or four slab-slices of thickly buttered saffron cake for brunch. Then it's almost always a large meat and potato pasty, or perhaps two, with brown sauce and red sauce – and maybe mustard – for lunch. On the afternoon tea plate, there would generally be two scones, sometimes three, with lashings of homemade jam and Kernish cream.'

Louis was already feeling sick at the thought of having to eat all that food every single day. But he listened politely as Mr Sand continued with enormous enthusiasm.

'In the early evening, a firm favourite for dinner is deep-fried, beer-battered fish 'n' chips, with tartar sauce and lots of salt and vinegar. And, finally, for supper, the best meal of the day in my opinion, a whole blue cheese round with a packet of cream crackers and a jar of homepickled onions.'

'I'm... I'm not sure I can eat all that...' began Louis, in defence of his stomach.

'Now, Your Young Highness, this is very important,' said Mr Sand, becoming very serious as he interrupted the worried boy with a halt of his hand. 'It is considered extremely rude to refuse food in Kernowland, the height of bad manners, especially if you are a guest. So, to be on the safe side, it's best to just say "yes" whenever offered food... even if you've only just eaten elsewhere.'

Louis' head dropped. He wanted to be polite and do the right thing, but he wasn't at all sure he could force down so much food.

'But there's no real need to worry,' continued Mr Sand, giving one of his big smiles whilst proudly patting his pot belly, 'you'll soon get used to it as your tummy expands.'

Despite Mr Sand's encouragement, Louis was still

worrying about how he could possibly eat all that food when, suddenly, as they were almost upon the castle, the rainbows vanished before his eyes.

'Where have all the rainbows gone?' he asked.

'Ah, they've switched the forcefield off,' informed Mr Sand. 'They've no doubt seen us coming.'

On reaching the moat, Lieutenant Liskeard raised his hand, and Louis, Mr Sand, Sergeant Stout, and the troop of soldiers all stopped.

Mrs Maggitt was mumble-worrying to herself in the gaol wagon. 'Oh, what's going to become of us?'

'Shut up, woman. That mouth of yours will hang us all,' complained her husband. 'Say nothing. Nothing!'

'Yeah. Nothing!' added Scurvy. 'Not a word... or it'll be your last. Only one more day to hold out and we'll all get what we've been promised. You'll be *Maggitt and Maggitt*, Kernowland's first slave auctioneers... And I'll be *Scurvy, Chief of Secret Police*. Got a ring to it, eh?'

'Yes, Mr Scurvy, yes indeed it has,' enthused Mr Maggitt.

'Well... my fellow conspirators,' continued Scurvy, 'you should know that the Guillotine of Sirap is already on its way. And the first thing I'm going to do in my new job after the invasion is to get rid of that meddlesome little prince, along with any other royals that have to go.'

'But why did you buy him, Mr Scurvy?' asked Mrs Maggitt. 'Surely not so you could simply lop his head off.'

'Wanted a slave boy. Any man in my new position would have to have at least one slave, to run and fetch and all that sort of thing. And he had good teeth. I had a tooth surgeon lined up for the extraction. I wanted his teeth. And I wanted a slave. That's why I bought him. But I'll get another slavekid. That one's nothing but trouble... and a little thief to boot. I'll make him give me back the

Young Master's key. Then I'll take his teeth. And then he's for the chop with the Guillotine of Sirap... or my name's not Sheviok Scurvy!'

Blissfully unaware of the conversation about his fate going on in the gaol wagon, Louis stared up at the two huge towers that flanked the entrance to the castle.

A great drawbridge hung at an angle between them, as if it was halfway up and halfway down. The thick chains holding the drawbridge creaked as it was lowered slowly to the ground, where it formed a safe crossing over the moat. Lieutenant Liskeard led the way over the drawbridge.

As they entered the castle through the imposing entrance, a little mouse scampered across their path.

Louis' thoughts returned to Misty.

He hoped and hoped that his little friend was all right.

THIRTY-ONE

Fat Cat

Meow was almost full up with all the morsels she had been given by the Eden visitors. She had, however, been very careful to leave just enough room for that rare delicacy in her diet: ice-mouse.

She made her way slowly back to the compost heap to check on her dessert. The fat cat, who prided herself on being quite nimble for her age and size, leapt straight on top of the steaming pile of rotting vegetation.

Although Meow had had the sense to put Misty on the compost heap to warm him through a bit, the little mouse was not surrounded by special warming leaves as Louis had been, so his thaw was taking quite a lot longer. One lick with her sandpaper tongue and a quick attempt at a crunch between her two rows of sharp teeth, was enough to tell her that the mouse *still* wasn't quite ready to eat.

I know, I'll warm it a little myself, thought the cat. Meow clawed at the surface of the compost heap all around Misty and padded around in a circle, as cats often seem to do when they are making a place on which to lie. Then she settled her fat body right down on top of the mouse and, despite the coldness of the icy little lump under her tummy, promptly fell fast asleep.

Misty was in darkness underneath the belly of the purring cat. His squashed lungs were straining for air. His tiny heart thumped and pounded. The little blue mouse began to panic. He was slowly suffocating.

THIRTY-TWO

Kernow Castle

Inquisitive soldiers in their hundreds peered over the ramparts of Kernow Castle. They all seemed extremely interested in visitors important enough for the Forcesphere test to be interrupted.

Louis looked all around him, up and down and from side to side. Everywhere there were defences, weapons, contraptions; things he had never seen before, nor even imagined. Lieutenant Liskeard issued his orders politely but firmly.

'Sergeant Stout, please take the prisoners to the castle keep for further questioning. I'll be along shortly.'

'My pleasure, sa!' barked the sergeant, throwing a look of contempt at Scurvy and the Maggitts in the gaol wagon.

The Lieutenant then escorted Louis and Mr Sand up some steps and through a grand arch, guarded on each side by a soldier with a musket over his shoulder. The prince and the surveyor followed on behind the officer as he led them down a long, wide passageway, with lots of portraits hung upon its walls.

'The *Corridor of the Ancestors*,' said Mr Sand with pride, as he saw his young charge taking an interest in the pictures. They are all the Kings and Queens who have ever sat on the throne of Kernowland.'

'They're all smiling... and they look very kind,' observed Louis.

'Oh yes, they certainly are. Or I should say, they *were*, since, being ancestors, they've all long since passed on to the Rainbow Realm. The Kings and Queens have always been very kind and gentle. They treat the people as if we are all one big family.' That's nice, thought Louis.

At the end of the corridor, they stopped in front of huge wooden doors. Lieutenant Liskeard halted, and swung around to face them.

'I have to take my leave here, Your Highness, Mr Sand. Duty calls. Slavers to question. Must dash.'

With a bow to Louis, and a nod to Mr Sand, he stood to attention, about-turned, stamped his foot and marched back down the corridor, the sound of his clicking heels getting ever fainter as he went.

'Thank you for rescuing me,' shouted Louis after him.

'We'll wait in the Welcome Hall,' said Mr Sand, as he ushered the young prince towards the doors.

'It's through here.'

Louis looked around the room that he and Mr Sand had just entered. It was large and circular with a very high ceiling. Looking up, he thought they might be at the bottom of the tall central tower he had seen from the hill. In addition to the main entrance through which they came in, there were twelve doors around the perimeter of the room. Mr Sand began to explain.

'This is the Welcome Hall. We're on the ground floor of the Dome Tower. Each of these twelve doors opens into a corridor which leads to one of the twelve spire towers. That archway leads to a spiral staircase which will take us to the upper floors of the Dome Tower.'

Just then, before Mr Sand could continue, a very tall, stick-thin man emerged through the archway. He was dressed in a black morning suit, with a gold waistcoat and a gold bow tie. The tails of the coat flapped behind him as he walked towards them. The man held his head very still and his back very straight, so that his nose stuck up in the air in a very superior pose. He seemed to be looking along his nose to navigate.

'Ah Pemberley, good to see you,' greeted Mr Sand when the man reached the bottom of the steps.

'You are most kind as always, sir,' replied the man, looking straight ahead at neither of them, and hardly moving his lips as he spoke.

'Can we go up?' asked Mr Sand.

'Yes sir. The King awaits his royal visitor in the Throne Room.' Inviting Louis to follow him, with a wave of his long thin arm, the man said: 'If it pleases you to follow me, Your Highness.'

With that, the man turned on his heels with the grace of a ballroom dancer and began to retrace his steps towards the arch. Louis began walking after him in as princely a fashion as he could manage.

He and Mr Sand followed the man at a distance. They began to climb a stone spiral staircase, which Louis imagined must be inside the walls of the Dome Tower.

'Mr Sand,' whispered Louis, so that the man in the suit wouldn't hear, 'who is Mr Pemberley?'

'He is the King's butler, Your Highness,' whispered his teacher. 'But you have to remember that he is a servant and you are a prince. You must never call him "Mr" Pemberley, or suspicions will be aroused about your royal pedigree. Come to think of it, you should, from this moment on, call me by my second name only when other people are around. Go on, try it now.'

Louis hesitated.

'Okay... Sand, I understand.' He felt uncomfortable talking to Mr Sand like that, but he understood why he had to do it.

'Very good, Your Highness. I know it's hard, but you must also make every effort to remember all I have told you about Kernowland and Erthwurld and how to behave as a Prince of Forestland. Only the King and I know your secret. No one else must suspect.

'I'll try my best,' promised Louis, though he was still a little daunted by the prospect of pretending to be a prince all the time.

'That's the spirit,' encouraged Mr Sand. 'We haven't got a lot of time and there's so much for you to learn. I'll have to instruct you on how to behave at the Midsummer's Eve Banquet Ball later tonight. And then there's tomorrow morning's White Light Ceremony as well. And all sorts of other things. Oh my, what a lot for a young man to learn in such a short time.'

'Yes,' agreed Louis, now doubly daunted by the prospect of assimilating all that knowledge and putting it in to action.

'You'll soon be learning quite a bit more about Kernowland and Erthwurld from the King,' said Mr Sand. 'And we'll also be showing you how we propose to rescue your sister.'

Being reminded of Tizzie made Louis a bit upset. He looked at the floor as little tears welled in his eyes. Mr Sand seemed to know what was wrong.

'It won't be long now,' he comforted. 'We can begin the rescue in a week or so. And then you can go home.'

A week!

THIRTY-THREE

King Kernow XXXIII

A week!

'Yes, but wouldn't it be better if we started today?' asked a worried Louis, as tentatively and politely as he could. He didn't want to be rude to Mr Sand, but he thought they could be getting on with the rescue a bit quicker than that.

'Oh my. There's so very much for you to learn about Kernowland and Erthwurld,' sighed Mr Sand. 'I keep forgetting that you know nothing of our ways and our magic. But, with all these new things, it is much easier for me to show rather than tell. All will be revealed in a few moments when you meet the King.'

After climbing a few more stone steps, Louis and Mr Sand followed Pemberley into the Throne Room. Lots of candle chandeliers were hanging from the very high ceiling.

'Permacandles. They're made from permawax,' informed Mr Sand, when he saw Louis staring at the bright, flickering lights. 'The wax never melts. The light never goes out.'

Louis looked around the room. There was a long red carpet in the centre, which led from the door all the way down the room and up three steps that rose to a stone platform, on which stood a grand throne, flanked by two huge Kernow flags.

On the throne sat a small, thin man with a golden crown on his head. In the centre of the crown, at the front, was a very large diamond, which glistened and sparkled. Smaller stones, in all the colours of the rainbow, were set around the crown.

Louis guessed this must be the King.

'May I present Prince Louis of Forestland, Your Majesty,' said Pemberley, bowing slightly to the King.

'Greetings to you and Forestland, Prince Louis,' said the King, warmly. 'I am King Kernow The Thirty-Third, and I bid you a very warm welcome to our castle and our country.'

He seems very nice, thought Louis, as he bowed in the way that Mr Sand had shown him.

'I am honoured to meet you, Your Majesty,' he said very politely, 'and thank you very much for sending your soldiers and Sand to rescue me.'

'Least I could do,' replied the King. 'That will be all, thank you, Pemberley.'

They all watched the butler leave. As Pemberley departed, King Kernow XXXIII stood up and walked down the few steps to the red carpet on which Louis and Mr Sand were standing.

'Now we can talk openly,' he said to Louis, putting his arm around the boy's shoulder. 'I am terribly sorry to hear of your troubles in our land and also that your sister was kidnapped and sold to the pirates.

'I should say, before we go any further, that nearly all of the Kernowfolk are gentle and peaceful and good. You were very unlucky to meet that would-be child-slaver, Melanchol Drym, and his accomplices.'

Louis smiled and gave a little shrug.

'I must also say, both Sand I feel personally responsible for bringing you here to Kernowland and Erthwurld. We want to help you return home as soon as possible. But, of course, we need to find and rescue your sister first.

'And, in that regard, I'd imagine Sand has been telling you something about map reading and navigation?'

The expression on Louis' face showed the King that

this was indeed the case.

'And *Zooming Maps* and *Golden Chambers*, have you been learning about them too?'

Louis looked blank.

'Haven't had time for those particular lessons, Your Majesty,' said Mr Sand. 'Thought it best to wait... to show rather than tell.'

'Yes, much easier with such new and complicated ideas,' agreed the King.

'And there's no time like the present... let's go to the Map Room right now.'

THIRTY-FOUR

The Map Room

The King led Louis and Mr Sand out of the Throne Room. They spiralled up the stone steps to the next floor of the Dome Tower, where they entered the Map Room. There were maps everywhere; maps all around the walls, maps in frames suspended on cords from the ceiling, even a map covering the middle of the floor. The King ushered Louis over to a huge parchment map on the wall.

'As you can see, it's a map of Kernowland. Here's Towan Blystra, and there's Polperro, and Eden Valley, and so on. Looks pretty ordinary doesn't it?' Louis nodded. 'But there is something very special about this map... it's a zooming map. Which means – and this is the clever bit – if you put your finger on any part of the parchment... the map "zooms in".' Louis watched as the King touched the map. It zoomed, so that the point he was touching got bigger and bigger.

'If we zoom in far enough, we can just about see people,' continued the King. 'Look, there, on the road to Eden Valley... I'd bet my crown that's Bartholomew Bude, our head gardener, on his way to collect the castle compost in his cart.'

'He doesn't seem to be moving,' observed Louis.

'Quite correct. We get snapshots, not real-time images,' replied the King. 'Can't see him moving because the map only updates once an hour. That's all our *eyes in the skies* can manage at the moment... one image per hour.'

'What are eyes in the skies, Your Majesty?' asked Louis.

'Why, *space orbiters* of course.'

'*Satellites* to you, Prince Louis,' helped Mr Sand.

'Yes, satellites,' agreed the King. 'You'll have to forgive me, haven't spent any time in your world. Right, let's get back to the map. Here's Goonhilly. It's our main technical, scientific, and inventing facility. Some time ago, the boffins and mutationeers down there grew a clear silicon crystal sphere around a large animal eye. After a few modifications, they found that the silicon crystal could work as a brain for the eye. It could actually see! Well, it was soon realised that the seeing spheres had a number of applications, one of which was space orbiters.'

'But how do they get the orbiters into space?' asked Louis.

'Oh, that's the easy part,' answered Mr Sand. 'We launch the spheres into orbit using a huge catapult, which has a very thick stretchy band made of the same material as your catapult. The band is stretched down a deep vertical mine shaft and then, when it's released, the power is sufficient to launch an orbiter in to space. The spheres are only as big as your head.' Louis' mind boggled as he tried to imagine this. He thought that only rockets could launch things into space.

'The spheres orbit the Erth, looking at everything below,' continued the King. 'At intervals of one hour, they send back images of what they see, which are carried on waves of light. The images are picked up by our big receiving dishes at Goonhilly, and then sent on over here so we can view them on this map. There's a receiving dish right at the top of this Dome Tower.'

Louis was fascinated by the zooming map and the eyes in the skies, but he couldn't see how they would help in the search for Tizzie: 'Your Majesty, this map is really interesting. But it's a map of Kernowland... and Tizzie's gone somewhere else. How will it help find her and rescue her?'

'Understand the question,' replied the King, 'just trying to explain one thing at a time...

'...Previously, we've only launched eyes in the skies that orbit in space above Kernowland and send back pictures of our own little country. However, we've just built a new prototype model of orbiter that can send back images of the other lands and seas of Erthwurld. It's part of the continuous improvements in our defences against the threat of invasion by Evile and his Empire. As soon as I learned about your predicament, I authorised Professor Mullion, the head man down at Goonhilly, to launch the new orbiter. We've called it *Rescuer*.

As the King explained, it started to dawn on Louis how *Rescuer* might be very useful in finding Tizzie.

'When we knew you and your sister had been taken to Polperro, it was likely that you'd be sold and taken away by sea. So we started looking there with *Rescuer* and spotted *The Revenger*, Captain Pigleg's ship. We've been tracking the ship's movements ever since. Pictures we've received show that *The Revenger* made its first stop for a short while in Port Ervahel, to pick up whalehorses.' Louis tried to imagine what a whalehorse looked like as the King continued.

'The boffins down at Goonhilly have also developed a portable version of the zooming map to work with *Rescuer*. And I'm glad to report that the map has been tested and activated, and it's ready for use. Professor Mullion delivered it personally this afternoon, just before you arrived. It's in this case.'

As he spoke, the King reached inside his garments and withdrew a thin, cylindrical case, which appeared to Louis to be made of brown leather. A brown strap, attached at either end, dangled down from the case. He took the top off it and pulled out a scroll of parchment tied with a ribbon.

'The Goonhilly boffins have called this map *Zoom*er,' continued the King. 'They like to give every piece of new technology a name, so they can identify it easily.' Unrolling the parchment, the King pointed to the map and said: 'It's a map of Erthwurld.' Louis scanned the map, noting the strange names as he did so. 'Acirfa', 'Eporue', 'Cificap Ocean'; all words he'd never seen before.

'Now, as I said, this new portable zooming map works specifically with *Rescuer*,' reminded the King. 'So, you can only see on *Zoomer* what *Rescuer* is seeing from the sky. We would need to send up a lot more orbiting eyes to see everything that's going on all over Erthwurld, but this is a good start. So, if I touch the map here, just southwest of Port Ervahel, we can see there are a number of tiny ships shown on the map. And if we zoom in on them one at a time, we can confirm which is *The Revenger*.'

'How can you tell?' asked Louis, as he looked at all the little ship-dots on the map. From high above, they all looked the same.

'Well, if we zoom right in, we can generally make out the flag at the top of the mast,' answered the King. 'And you certainly can't mistake Pigleg's flag, the *Jolly Grunter*.' Louis had heard of a *Jolly Roger* pirate's flag, which was normally black with a white grinning human skull and two white bones forming a cross on it. But he'd never heard of a *Jolly Grunter*. Whilst Louis was thinking, the King was using *Zoomer* to search for the *The Revenger*.

'There!' he declared, after a few moments. 'Pigleg's flag! Black with white grinning boar's skull and two boar's leg bones in the shape of a cross.'

Louis looked. He was fascinated that *Zoomer* could see such detail.

'That image is less than an hour old,' informed the King, as he rolled *Zoomer* up and put it back in its case. 'Unless your sister was offloaded at Port Ervahel, which is pretty unlikely given our intelligence, she's on that ship.'

Louis was momentarily elated to think that Tizzie's whereabouts had been discovered. However, his joy soon turned to uncertainty once more. How would knowing where she was help in actually rescuing her?

'But how... ' he began to ask the question.

'Ahead of you,' interrupted the King. 'Sand, I do believe the young prince is ready to see the secret beneath the Mosaic Map.'

THIRTY-FIVE

The Ten

Clevercloggs was scanning the pages of the diary as he rode along on Heavyfeather. He was deciphering as fast as his huge brain could go.

'We must decode as much as possible so that the King can act swiftly,' he said to Dribble. To help in his task, Clevercloggs had written out the whole code on more graph paper.

'Look,' he showed Dribble, 'an **A** written down in the diary stands for a *Z*, and a **B** stands for an A and so on.'

A	B	C	D	E	F	G	H	I
Z	*A*	*B*	*C*	*D*	*E*	*F*	*G*	*H*
J	K	L	M	N	O	P	Q	R
I	*J*	*K*	*L*	*M*	*N*	*O*	*P*	*Q*
S	T	U	V	W	X	Y	Z	
R	*S*	*T*	*U*	*V*	*W*	*X*	*Y*	

Dribble glanced at the graph paper being held in front of him. It wasn't as if he could help much as he couldn't read or write, but he was very pleased that Clevercloggs was including him.

Clevercloggs continued working through the diary. He started at the top of a page where Dribble's drool had made the ink run at the bottom.

'Let's see. The title appears to be written using the same code, he mused, before reading the letters aloud. '**U,** that stands for *T,* then **I,** which is really *H,* then **F,** that's *E.* Then there's a space before, **U-F-O.**'

'*THE TEN,*' he declared, as he wrote it down quickly.

He really is very clever, thought Dribble.

Continuing to read the same page whilst riding along, Clevercloggs suddenly declared: 'Aha! I think this is a list of names.

ESZN

NBHHJUU

NBHHJUU

TDVSWZ

XFOESPO

XBSMFHHBO

'Oh, dear me,' he said, as, one by one, he wrote down the real names of each person on the list on his graph paper. After decoding the names, Clevercloggs returned to the intriguing title at the top of the page.

'The Ten?' he pondered. 'That surely means there are ten names. And it certainly appears that more names were written on that list. But unfortunately, after the first six, I'm afraid they're all smudged.

'Nevertheless, I think we could safely say that, as well as the three traitors back at Washaway, and the three we've just found out about from the list, there are probably at least four more traitors.

'And we know there's an invasion planned. But when? And what does "Darkness Day" mean?'

With that, he buried his head in the diary once again, as he desperately tried to find out more.

THIRTY-SIX

Princess Satnohacop

Dribble was tired as they stopped at the water well in the village of Indian Queens.

'Now, Dribble, there was a reason for coming this way,' said Clevercloggs. 'You wait here; I need to go to that inn.'

Dribble wondered whether it was the right time for the old gnome to be having ale. However, instead of going in to the inn, Clevercloggs pulled himself from Heavyfeather's back and sat on a seat outside. He asked a waitress for something.

Then another person came out; a beautiful young woman in a barmaid's dress. Clevercloggs spoke to her. Dribble noticed that, whilst the old gnome was talking to the young woman, he was writing a note, which he then handed over. She looked at the note, appearing to be very worried by it, before hurrying off back into the inn.

Clevercloggs hobbled back to the well to explain.

'That's Princess Satnohacop. Her father, Chief Natahwop, is the leader of the Redskins of Acirema North. The Chief has to do what Evile says, for the sake of his people. But I know that he secretly hates what Evile is doing to Erthwurld. He would like to unite the people of Acirema North against the Empire. He's the sort of leader who could do it.

'The Princess escaped to Kernowland when Acirema was invaded ten years ago. She has been living and working as a barmaid as part of her cover, a disguise in case Evile's spies are watching. Like me, she's a member of the resistance.'

Dribble looked admiringly at Clevercloggs as the old gnome continued.

'It's a long shot, but we have to try everything. The future of the whole wurld is at stake. I've given her a note for her father. It explains the contents of the diary that I've been able to work out so far. The princess is very brave. She's going to return to Acirema North and take the note to the Chief herself, to see if he can help Kernowland.'

Moments later, Princess Satnohacop came out of the inn with her shawl draped over her shoulders and walked quickly to her lodgings across the village square.

Whilst they were still resting, the Princess emerged from the house again with a travelling bag in her hand. Clevercloggs waved and wished her a safe journey, before confiding his fears to Dribble.

'I hope she makes it to Falmouth Port in time to escape the invasion.'

THIRTY-SEVEN

The Mosaic Map

The King made his way towards the centre of the Map Room.

'This is the Mosaic Map,' he said, pointing to the floor. Looking down, Louis saw it was by far the largest map in the room. The map was at least ten of Louis' paces long and five wide. It was made up of hundreds of small square tiles, each about the size of a chessboard square.

'You'd better take over now, Sand. I've got another meeting in the Throne Room. Here's the key and *Zoomer*.' Mr Sand took the key and *Zoomer*, and the King then left them.

'As you can see, this mosaic is a large map of the whole of Erthwurld,' explained Mr Sand, as he walked on to the map. 'But *this* is a map with a secret.' Stopping suddenly, he beckoned to Louis to join him.

'Look here,' he continued, bending down and pointing to a single square tile on which was drawn the outline of Kernowland. 'This is the locktile. It's the only one that is not glued down.'

Mr Sand then pushed on the tile with his finger. To Louis' surprise, the tile popped open on a hinge which ran along one of its sides. Mr Sand pointed.

'When opened, the Kernowland locktile reveals the golden lock, which guards one of the Seven Wonders of Erthwurld. And, for a golden lock... we need a Golden Key.'

Mr Sand now had Louis' full attention. He was especially interested in the Golden Key that his teacher was holding. It looked just like the one that had dropped into the cellar at the Polperro Inn. It even had writing down the side.

Mr Sand inserted the Golden Key in the golden lock, turned it anti-clockwise, removed the key, lifted a little handle that surrounded the lock on another hinge, and then pulled. With that, a square trapdoor opened, its edges matched perfectly to some of the tile edges on the map. The open trapdoor revealed a square hole, just big enough for a man to get through.

'Those stone steps lead down to the Golden Cavern,' said Mr Sand.

'You go first.'

Louis put his foot on the first stone step. Mr Sand followed.

'I'll just close the mapdoor,' said his teacher, as they both got below floor level. 'The locktile on the map closes itself automatically. No one would know we're down here. It will be dark so we'll need this.'

From his pocket, he produced a yellow glow-crystal and tapped it lightly on the buckle of his belt. As the mapdoor closed shut above them, the little crystal started glowing and Louis could see around him. He counted twelve steps to the bottom of the staircase.

'We're between two floors of the Dome Tower,' explained Mr Sand. 'If we move along this passageway, we can use a secret spiral stairway that winds around inside the Dome Tower walls. It will take us down to the Golden Cavern, which is underground, directly below the Dome Tower.

They made their way quickly down the stone steps by the light of the glow-crystal. Suddenly, Louis noticed flickering shadows up ahead.

'What's that moving on the walls, Mr Sand?' he asked.

'Shadows from the permacandles that light the Golden Cavern,' answered Mr Sand.

Louis entered the cavern first. He was amazed by what he saw. The walls of the cavern shimmered in the glow of the permacandles. Gold nuggets and glistening green stones were peppered everywhere. Golden paving slabs led up to a circular rock in a recess on the opposite wall, which looked a bit like the Crystal Pool. But it was green not blue, and vertical not horizontal. There is so much to learn about Kernowland and Erthwurld, thought Louis... it might take forever.

Mr Sand led Louis along the golden slabs towards the green rock.

'This is *Godolphin's Crystal Door*,' he announced, rather grandly.

'We're going to use it to rescue your sister.'

THIRTY-EIGHT

The Crystal Door

Now they were getting somewhere. Louis was all ears as Mr Sand continued.

'From here, using the Crystal Door, we can travel all over Erthwurld in an instant.'

'But I still don't understand why we can't start now,' said Louis in a questioning tone, 'especially since we know where Tizzie is.'

'Well, that's what I've been leading up to with all these lessons,' said Mr Sand. 'I thought it best to show you in stages to help you understand. It'll help to look at *Zoomer*.'

Mr Sand then removed *Zoomer* from its leather case and handed it to his pupil saying: 'If you could just hold *Zoomer* open.' Louis took the zooming map, unrolled it and held it open. He looked at the map of Erthwurld on the parchment as Mr Sand explained.

'Now, as the King said, we're pretty sure that Tizzie is on *The Revenger*, and the ship has been to Port Ervahel for whalehorses. We also know, from *Zoomer*, that the pirate ship is currently off the coast of Ecnarf, being pulled at high speed on a south westerly course. Then they'll probably hug the coast of Lagutrop as they head further south towards the continent of Acirfa.'

'How do you know they're going there?' asked Louis.

'We can be fairly sure they're making for Jungleland in Acirfa,' answered Mr Sand confidently. 'Every year, at around this time, Captain Pigleg heads for Jungleland with a cargo of child-bait, in a quest for revenge on Big Red

Grunter, the boar that took his leg. Assuming that's the case, the pirates will almost certainly stop at various places along the way, to collect more slaves and anything else they need for the boar hunt. Possible ports of call on the way are Ratlarbig Rock, Acnalbasac City and Airanac Narg, one of the Isles of Airanac. Once they reach the port city of Lujnab, on the west coast of Acirfa, I'd imagine they'll take in more hunt provisions and then sail up the River Aibmag, to Nwotegroeg, the last port town capable of docking a sea-going vessel. Then they'll leave the ship and go into the jungle on the hunt for Big Red Grunter.

'The reason we're not leaving now is that, even if they stop for a while at any or all of these places, it won't be for long, so we'd do much better to wait and go straight to Jungleland. We can use the Crystal Door to arrive just before they do. So, hopefully, you'll now understand why there would be absolutely no point in us starting the rescue until they get to their ultimate destination.'

'Yes, I see now,' agreed Louis.

'To make sure we get the timing right, we'll get regular intelligence reports from our contacts in *RAE*, to corroborate the sightings with *Zoomer*.'

'What's "ray"?' asked Louis.

'Rebels Against Evile,' answered Mr Sand. 'The resistance fighters take on Evile's Empire wherever and whenever they can around the wurld. We are in constant contact with them, and do whatever we can to help in the cause of wiping the Emperor's evil regime from the face of the Erth.'

Louis was glad to think there were other people in Erthwurld who were standing up for Right and Good.

'But rest assured,' continued Mr Sand, 'we will begin the rescue at the earliest possible time using the Crystal Door.'

'Thanks, Mr Sand,' said Louis gratefully. 'Can you tell me how the door works?'

'Erth Magic,' explained Mr Sand. 'Powerful Erth Magic from Godolphin. Having decided where we want to go, we simply put one hand on the door and say our destination out loud. We must be careful to say the address in the correct order, of course, so that we don't end up in the wrong place. Name of town first, then country, then sector, then continent. So, when the time comes, we'll probably say, "Nwotegroeg, Aibmag, Jungleland, Acirfa".'

Louis repeated the address in his head, trying to memorise it. That was one address he knew he shouldn't forget.

'Godolphin ensured that the arrival points in or near the towns are in safe places, like caves or forest clearings,' continued Mr Sand. 'Wouldn't want to arrive the other end in the middle of an enemy stronghold, would we!?'

Shaking his head to show his agreement, the young boy then had to ask about something that he couldn't quite work out: 'But, if we go such a long way away in an instant... how do we get back?'

THIRTY-NINE

The Spare Golden Key

Good question,' said Mr Sand, as he reached in his pocket for something.

'Well, Godolphin had thought about this, and that's why he embedded a small clear crystal in the end of the Golden Key that opens the mapdoor on the Mosaic Map. He did the same with the spare.'

Louis looked closely at the key that his teacher was holding. There was a very small glistening crystal in the end of it.

'You simply have to touch the crystal end of the key on any natural part of the Erth – that is the water, sand, rocks, or ground, wherever you are on the planet – and you will be transported back here. Of course, you don't want to do it accidentally, so you need a Half-Lock Spell as well.

'The spell is written along the key. But those words are only half of what you need, hence the name. So, to make it work, you have to say the words on the key first. Can you read them?

'*Golden Cavern*', read Louis.

'That's right. And then you must remember to say, "*by the power of Godolphin*", straight afterwards. As soon as you say that, you will be instantly returned here.'

'That's magic!' exclaimed Louis.

'Precisely,' agreed Mr Sand.

'From time to time, people like Godolphin the Great are born who bring us new things that are beyond our understanding. We know the new things work, but we don't know how. We call them "magic" because of this. Of course, as soon as we understand *how* magic works, it doesn't seem magical anymore. Then we call it "science", and we can do or make the things over and over again.'

Louis nodded to show he understood as Mr Sand continued.

'Of course, we'd like to have lots of Golden Keys so that more people can use them. One key has only got enough power to bring back six people at a time. Everyone has to be touching the person holding the key if they want to be transported back to the cavern. So, if we want to bring them all back at the same time, including your sister, we can only take a rescue party of five on our search for Tizzie.

'This is quite inconvenient. That's why they've got the spare key down at Goonhilly. The scientists are trying to find out how it works, so that we can make some copies. Then lots more people would be able to use the Crystal Door. It's top secret, so only Professor Mullion and his assistant, Dr Lizard, know about it.'

Louis was concentrating hard, trying to take everything in. He thought it was now time to tell Mr Sand something.

'You know you said there are two keys...' he began.

'Yes, ' said Mr Sand.

'And the other Golden Key is at this Goonhilly place?'

'That's right.'

'It's just that, I think I've seen another key, exactly like this one.'

Mr Sand smiled as if Louis was very much mistaken.

'Oh no,' he said with confidence, 'the spare key is currently at Goonhilly.'

Louis wasn't so sure. He still thought this Golden Key

was identical to the one he'd seen at the Polperro Inn, but his thoughts were interrupted as Mr Sand spoke again.

'Let's put *Zoomer* in its case. We'll leave it here, just in front of the Crystal Door, ready for when we go through. It will be safe in the cavern.'

Louis rolled up the map and put it in its case as Mr Sand carried on speaking.

'I've been thinking about who we will take with us. There are three other places. Lieutenant Liskeard is a good man; I'd like to take him along.'

'Yes, me too,' nodded Louis enthusiastically. He liked Lieutenant Liskeard.

'Well, we've still got some time to pick the rescue team,' said Mr Sand. 'But, right now, we've got a Midsummer's Eve Grand Banquet Ball to prepare for.

'Which means more lessons, I'm afraid.'

FORTY

Mrs Portwrinkle

After returning to the Welcome Hall from the Golden Cavern, Louis and Mr Sand were soon walking along a corridor. They passed a sign, in the form of a white-gloved fist, which had a finger pointing forwards. The sign said: *Mrs Portwrinkle's Kitchen.*

The smells coming from the kitchen were fantastic. Louis could hear a very jolly – and extremely loud – voice, shouting orders.

'I don't want to confuse you,' continued Mr Sand, 'but, although Mrs Portwrinkle has never been married, everyone, even the King, calls her "Mrs" as a sign of respect for her genius. So, remember to refer to Pemberley without the "Mr", but it's always *Mrs* Portwrinkle.'

'I'll try,' said Louis, as Mr Sand continued.

'Mrs Portwrinkle is such a good cook that people can't get enough of her recipes. You'll no doubt remember we had a *Mrs Portwrinkle Pasty* down at Eden Valley, but there's a whole range of her food to enjoy. I can't wait for the Banquet Ball!'

As they entered Mrs Portwrinkle's domain, she bustled over to them, her arms open wide. Louis saw she was very short, extremely plump and, rather than a chef's hat, wore a frilly white bonnet over her short, straight, black hair. Her long white apron was spotlessly clean.

She also wore what Louis thought his nan might call 'sensible' boots, which came halfway up her shins to meet the apron hem.

'I heard you were coming, Your Little Highness,' said Mrs Portwrinkle warmly, as she pulled Louis towards her and smothered his head in her ample bosom.

'Welcome. Welcome. Welcome.'

The hug was so firm that Louis thought he might stop breathing if it went on too long. After the hug, Mrs Portwrinkle showed them around the kitchen, with Louis learning all sorts of things as they went.

Pemberley arrived in the kitchen. He and Mrs Portwrinkle were informed by Mr Sand that it was the young prince's first ball and that he needed to know 'the necessaries'. The cook and the butler instructed Louis in the correct use of the cutlery for a twelve course grand banquet meal, as well how to use his napkin, which glass to drink from, and all sorts of other things he had to know in order to behave according to the expected royal protocol.

After about an hour of lessons and tests, they declared him 'ready'.

FORTY-ONE

The Midsummer's Eve Ball

Louis had learned that all sorts of people would be arriving from all over Kernowland for the Midsummer's Eve Banquet Ball.

Mr Sand had told him what would be happening during the evening and what he had to do. He had a list in his pocket, to help him remember. The first thing on the list was 'Meet and Greet' the guests, which is what he was going to do very shortly.

But before that, he had to briefly meet the other members of the Royal Family, who also lived in the castle.

'This is my lovely wife, Queen Agnes,' said the King, introducing Louis to a very large, jolly lady.

'Oh how lovely. A little royal munchkin to go with my big royal munchkin,' chuckled the Queen, as she bore down on Louis with her huge arms outstretched and her plump purple lips puckered in readiness for a big squelchy kiss.

Louis couldn't get away. The Queen soon had him in a bear hug and lifted him off the ground. She kissed him squarely on the lips. Urgghh! He felt her bristling moustache tickling his nose. Thankfully, it was only a brief kiss.

The King laughed heartily and made little jokes as he continued the brief introductions.

'And this is my daughter, Princess Kea,' he said proudly. 'Sweet sixteen last week. You'll be sitting next to her this evening.'

'Hello, Prince Louis,' said Princess Kea. With her kind blue eyes and long black hair, Louis thought she was quite probably the most beautiful girl he had ever seen.

'And here's my nephew, Prince Manaccan, eighteen tomorrow, a man at last,' said the King, before crossing the room to speak to Pemberley. Mr Sand had already told Louis that Prince Manaccan's father, the King's younger twin brother by five minutes, had died in an unfortunate accident in the woods a year ago, whilst out riding with his son.

'Hello, cousin,' said Prince Manaccan, with what Louis thought might be the faintest sneer. 'Not heard of you before. But then we royals can't possibly know all our *minor* cousins, can we?' Louis wasn't sure he liked the way Prince Manaccan talked to him. He was glad that was the only conversation they had time for before the royals had to begin their Meet & Greet duties.

Standing in line with the other members of the Royal Family, Louis watched as two soldiers checked people's invitations as they entered the Welcome Hall. Louis shook hands with each of them after they had bowed or curtsied to him.

Gong!

After everyone had arrived, a loud gong sounded and Pemberley made an announcement: 'Your Royal Highnesses, My Lords, Bards, Ladies and Gentlemen... dinner is served.'

In the Banquet Ballroom, everyone sat down at long tables, which were set out along the edges of the room, leaving a large space in the middle for the 'Entertainments' and 'Dancing' that were also on Louis' list for later in the evening.

The young prince sat down with Princess Kea on his right, and an elderly woman called Lady Lostwithiel on his left. As he feared, there were twelve courses on the menu. Louis was absolutely certain he wouldn't be able to eat it all. A plethora of cutlery on the table challenged Louis' memory. He tried to remember which knife, fork, or spoon to use from what Pemberley and Mrs Portwrinkle had taught him.

Princess Kea was very sweet, although it seemed to Louis that, for some reason, she was not very favourably disposed to Prince Manaccan, who sat on the other side of her. She completely ignored her first cousin, instead chatting to Louis about all sorts of subjects. Although he tried his hardest to remember all the things he'd learned about Forestland, Kernowland, and Erthwurld, Louis mostly listened rather than talked, in an attempt not to give anything away. And, to his own surprise, he managed to finish every bit of food that was put in front of him.

After dinner, the 'Entertainments' included jesters and tumblers, and all sorts of other fun. The finale was the *Kernowland Children's Choir*. A boy of about six – who was introduced as 'Tommy Tremar, the Tiny Treble of Towan Blystra' – sang a beautiful solo.

Louis had really enjoyed the evening up to this point, but was now so tired that he was glad when it was time for bed. Because of his age, he was going early, before the dancing started.

'Goodnight, Prince Louis,' said Mr Sand, who was just about to dance with his companion for the evening, a lady of about his own age. Louis had learned her name was, Miss Prudent, and that she was the headmistress of Tommy Tremar's school.

'I'll ask Pemberley to make sure you're awake early in the morning. We have to be up in good time for the White Light Ceremony.'

FORTY-TWO

The Ramdragons of Selaw

Madog The Slaughterer was the Chief of The Shlew, a fearsome race of warriors whose country, Selaw, lay to the north of Kernowland, on the far side of the Lotsirb Channel.

Madog had been delighted to be chosen by Evile to lead the first airborne wave of the invasion. This was his chance to show what the Ramraiders of Selaw could do.

The Ramraiders were mustering their forces, preparing for an attack on Kernowland. They flew into battle on red ramdragons. These were red dragons with huge curved rams' horns grown on their heads for battering with, the result of some simple mutationeering. Beneath the early morning mist, the cliff top was alive with roaring ramdragons, each with two pillars of smoke rising from its nostrils.

Madog pulled on his sheepskin coat and bronze ramhelmet, which had two rams' horns sticking out of it. Two of Madog's fiercest warriors, Hywel The Cleaver and Owain The Slayer, did likewise, in readiness for take-off.

'Get those ramdragons off the ground and in the air now,' shouted Madog at the top of his voice. 'I want to see the sky red with ramdragons.' With that, the leader of the Ramraiders threw his hairy leg over his black saddle and kicked his spurs into the red hide of his ramdragon, Dracoola, whose name was carved into a black leather collar around his neck.

'Roarrrhhhh!'

Dracoola roared as he felt the spurs bite. He puffed out short breaths of fire as he began running on all four legs, accelerating towards the cliff top at incredible speed. In less than ten paces the huge red beast was off the ground. He soared into the air, his long red neck stretching skyward.

Like most of the other ramdragons, Dracoola carried a blazebomb under his belly, in a big leather pouch tied around his body with ropes. Lots of practice meant that each ramdragon could set light to the blazebomb with a firebreath, just as the bundle of sticks and stones and gunpowder fell to erth when released from the pouch.

Morgan The Destroyer, Madog's second in command, and his ramdragon, Drilla, were next off the ground

'Haarrrhhhh!' he shouted, as Drilla soared upwards. Morgan loved flying on his ramdragon. He kicked his spurs twice into Drilla's leathery hide, and Drilla roared a breath of fire.

The nine biggest ramdragons were the last to take off. Known as 'cage carriers', they had thick ropes around their necks and hind quarters. As they ran towards the cliff top, the ropes uncoiled until becoming taut. Each rope was attached to a cage. The cages were dragged along the ground towards the cliff edge. Each cage contained something truly terrifying: a troglodyte.

Bred in the caves of Abuc, these beasts were part ape, part troll, and a very small part human. The human cells used to grow them were taken from the worst criminals that Evile's mutationeers could find in the darkest dungeons of the Empire. The mutant creatures were known around the wurld as 'trogs'.

None of the trogs was amused to be bumped and bounced along the ground. They shook and chewed the bars of the cages and shrieked with rage.

'Trroggaarhh! Trroggaarhh! Trroggaarhh!'

It was a deafening sound. Chewing the bars exposed the sharp teeth at the front of their mouths. All troglogdytes had this feature. The teeth were so distinctive that they even had a name: 'tearing teeth'. With these terrible weapons, trogs could tear a victim apart in seconds, especially if they were made razor sharp with a file. Morgan had handed each trog a file the evening before. Trogs weren't very clever, but they had worked out that every time they were given a file in the evening, they would be feasting on flesh the next day; and they had spent much of the night sharpening their tearing teeth. Madog had ordered that the trogs should not be fed for two weeks before the invasion, to make them especially hungry.

As each of the nine biggest ramdragons took off from the cliff top in turn, the cages were pulled over the edge. Suddenly, the trogs were flying too! They all stopped shrieking and looked at each other, somewhat bemused. None of them had ever been flying before.

When the whole squadron was in the air, it was a scary sight. More than two hundred ramdragons, each with a fearsome Shlew Ramraider sitting in a black saddle on its back, flapped their leathery wings in unison. Breaths of fire belched from their great mouths. Nine of the dragons had carry cages hanging from their necks. Each cage contained a half-starved trog, rattling and gnawing at the bars.

Morgan loved fighting, and this was going to be the biggest battle the wurld had seen for a very long time. He looked across and shouted at Madog as the ramdragon squadron levelled off above the sea.

'Next stop... Kernowland!'

FORTY-THREE

Skotos

Clevercloggs and Dribble had travelled through another night. The sun was rising in the east.

As he rode along on Heavyfeather, the wise old gnome was telling the dust dog more about what was in the diary.

'It mentions *Skotos* here in the same line as "Midsummer's Morning". The ancient legend of *Skotos* tells the story of Devillian, the Lord of Darkwurld, who used all his dark powers to send an instrument of darkness from Darkwurld to Erthwurld. Blacker than jet, *Skotos* was formed from a very dark and dense material, *darkite*, which is not of this Erth.

'*Skotos* was said to have manifested down in the deepest mines of Silom – one of the Islands of Eceerg – where it has lain undisturbed, waiting for the time when it could be used in the final great battle between Darkness and Light.

'No bigger than a marble, but weighing more than you, Dribble, the legend said that *Skotos* could magnify the power of a Dark Magician many times, and, if the magician was evil enough, be used to create the Dark Beam, which drains living things of their life-light in an instant. For this reason, *Skotos* is often referred to as the "Death Stone".

'But I thought it was just a story told by the ancients to frighten their children. Dark Magicians have often searched for *Skotos*, but it has never been found. So, why would Drym write about *Skotos*, the Death Stone, in this diary, right next to "Midsummer's Morning", "Invasion", and "Darkness Day"?'

Dribble didn't know the answer. But there was one thing for certain... if it was in *Drym's Diary*, it was sure to be bad news for someone.

'We need to hasten to Kernow Castle,' continued Clevercloggs. 'I don't like the sound of this *Skotos*. The White Light Ceremony takes place this very morning. I think that's when the traitors are planning to strike.'

FORTY-FOUR

Dark Magic

On Midsummer's morning, Louis rose early. After breakfast in bed, he put on his uniform and cape so that he was smartly dressed for the White Light Ceremony.

He then made his way down a long corridor, arriving in the Welcome Hall to meet Mr Sand as planned. Mr Sand told him something about the background to the ceremony he was just about to witness.

'The White Light Ceremony takes place in the Prism Chamber at the top of the Dome Tower. You should know a little about the history of magic and the Rainbow Wizards before we go up there. I'll explain very briefly, although there's a lot more to it than I can tell you in a few minutes.'

Louis nodded to show he was listening as Mr Sand continued.

'By performing dark rituals and practices, the bad people amongst the ancients made contact with Devillian, the Dark Lord of Darkwurld.

'The most evil of Devillian's servants became Dark Magicians. Dark Magic is the easiest to perform. It destroys and demolishes and hurts. Dark Magic was practiced for eons by the bad people of all tribes, who used it to enslave and dominate their fellow men and women and so bring Devillian's evil and darkness into Erthwurld from Darkwurld.

'But all Devillian's minions learned that there was a heavy price to pay for the worldly trinkets they received from him. The Dark Lord feeds on fear and chaos and death. He demanded total obedience and greater and greater sacrifices of pain and blood. His servants were expected to give over their whole lives to satisfy his insatiable hunger and lust. Throughout history, terrible things have been done in his name.

'It was Devillian's servants who created the conditions that led to the horrors of the Science Wars.

'Then, rising like a hissing serpent from the ashes of those horrible wars, came Evile, the Dark Lord's most devoted servant.'

Louis was just a little bit scared by what he was hearing, as Mr Sand continued to tell him more.

'For the first thousand years of his reign of terror, Evile spread darkness, slavery, fear, and death throughout the wurld, in an endless quest to feed Devillian's thirst for pain and blood. The forces of Darkness looked set to conquer Erthwurld, and resistance seemed hopeless.

'But all was not lost.'

FORTY-FIVE

Rainbow Magic

'For, right at the last moment, the prayers of the enslaved and oppressed and the good were answered. One had been born in Kernowland who could use the powers of Nature in a magical way in the cause of Right and Good. His name was Godolphin, the White Light Wizard.

'One night, the young Godolphin had a dream. A tree spoke to him. The tree said: *I am Nohwyn. My roots are in Erthwurld and my branches spread into the Rainbow Realm. I am the bridge. I know you have a question. Ask and I will tell, for I am the Tree of Knowing.*

'"How can I do more Good and Right and help the wurld?" asked Godolphin.

You have gained the knowledge, said Nohwyn. *You have acquired the wisdom. You have love in your heart. Knowledge. Wisdom. Love. These are the Three Qualities necessary to create White Light Magic. Tomorrow, you will point your wand and say,* "To the Highest Good, in the name of Omni", *and the White Beam of The One Light will shine from your wand.*

'The next day, Godolphin did as he was told in the dream. The White Beam of The One Light shined from his wand. The One Light created great miracles over many years.

'Godolphin's fame grew as news of his magical powers spread. At the very mention of his name, the servants of the Dark Lord retreated into the shadows. Evile bided his time, sipping his daily dose of the elixir that keeps him young.

137

'Inevitably, after a long life full of healing and helping people, Godolphin became old. He began to teach apprentices. But he found that others did not have his natural talent for White Light Magic. None could produce the White Beam of The One Light.

'So, to make his magical knowledge easier to share, Godolphin divided up what he knew into seven forms. Each form was assigned a colour of the spectrum, or ray of the rainbow. He called the whole, Rainbow Magic, and his apprentices became known as Rainbow Wizards. Rainbow Magic creates and builds and helps. It takes a lot of practice and skill and is much harder to do than Dark Magic.

'Every Rainbow Wizard studied all the seven rays of Rainbow Magic, but, since there was so much to learn, they could only specialise in one ray at a time.

'Godolphin was now near the end of his life, and he saw the danger ahead. Evile had conquered the lands and seas all around Kernowland and was getting stronger by the year. Kernowland was the last place left on Erth that was still untouched by his darkness. The Emperor had heard many tales of the power of the White Beam of The One Light and he dared not invade whilst Godolphin was in Kernowland. He continued to wait patiently, for time to rid him of the White Light Wizard.

'Then Godolphin had a second dream about Nowhyn. The Tree of Knowing said: *You have a question. Ask.*

'"If no other wizard can produce the White Beam, how will Kernowland be protected from Evile and his hordes when I am gone?" asked Godolphin.

'Nohwyn said: *One day, another may be born who has enough of the Three Qualities to produce the White Beam of The One Light on his or her own. But, for now, none of your apprentices is ready to be granted that awesome power. So, tomorrow, you will find the Prism of The One Light, a gift from the Rainbow Realm. It is the means to make the White Beam from the Seven Rays. If they work as a team, the Rainbow Wizards can use the Prism to create the White Beam of The One Light. Teamwork is the key.*

'Sure enough, when Godolphin awoke, he found a prism in his bed chamber, a gift from the Rainbow Realm. He taught the Rainbow Wizards to use it. They called it *Godolphin's Prism.*

'When Godolphin died, there was much sadness and much fear.

'But Evile, who had now learned of the power of Godolphin's Prism, still dared not invade. Even in death, the White Light Wizard, Godolphin the Great, had thwarted the Dark Lord's most devoted servant. And that is why, once every year, we have the White Light Ceremony; to create the White Beam of The One Light once more, and so keep Kernowland protected from the Darkness that hangs like a thick cloud over the rest of Erthwurld.

'I'm afraid that's all we've got time for now, Prince Louis. Come on, we don't want to be late for the ceremony.'

FORTY-SIX

Godolphin's Prism

Louis and Mr Sand walked up lots of stone steps. As they rounded the last curve of the spiral, Mr Sand breathed heavily before speaking.

'We're right at the top of the Dome Tower. Through those doors is the Prism Chamber, where the ceremony will take place.'

Louis followed his mentor through the doors, past four guards. The room was a bit like a small, round theatre, with rising benches built around a central circular stage.

Louis had learned earlier that he was to sit with the Royal Family in the front row, with Mr Sand directly behind him. He had also learned that, apart from Rainbow Wizards and the Royal Family, there would be a number of other people at the ceremony. Among these others were the two scientists from Goonhilly, Professor Mullion and Dr Lizard.

The King and Queen sat next to each other, in two seats bigger than the rest. Princess Kea sat on the right of the King. Prince Manaccan sat on the left of the Queen. Louis took his allotted seat next to Princess Kea and surveyed the room. On the stage was a rainbow-shaped table, divided into seven segments, each a different colour of the spectrum. Each of the seven segments had a small hollow in its surface. There were seven chairs, a red chair for the red segment of the table, an orange chair for the orange segment and so on. The inner curve at the front of the table faced a clear, pyramid-shaped object.

'That's Godolphin's Prism,' whispered Mr Sand. 'It merges the Seven Rays into the White Beam of The One Light, which reflects off the mirror and beams into the crystal generator, which is that clear crystal sphere hanging above our heads. This one annual conjoining of the wizards generates enough energy in the crystal generator for it to be able to power the Forcesphere for a year.

'During the ceremony, the Rainbow Wizards use all their concentration and power to generate the White Beam of The One Light. The success of the whole ceremony depends on them uniting and working together as a team.'

Not for the first time since he had arrived in this strange land, Louis was struggling to take everything in. There was such a lot to learn.

Three loud gongs rang out.

Gong! Gong! Gong!

FORTY-SEVEN

Rainbow Wizards

A long procession of men entered the Prism Chamber, five abreast, all chanting in a language Louis didn't understand. The sound made his body tingle. He felt a little light-headed. The men were all wearing long robes. Louis thought the robes were very much like long monk's habits, but instead of being brown, they were all the colours of the rainbow.

'Ordinary Rainbow Wizards,' whispered Mr Sand in his ear.

Louis counted them. Thirty-five in all. The five at the front wore red, the next five wore orange and so on.

Following on behind, again walking side by side, were more chanting wizards, except that, now, they were boy-wizards. The six boys, who were all aged around twelve or thirteen as far as Louis could make out, were wearing six colours of the rainbow. Louis quickly noticed that the red one was missing.

'Apprentices,' said Mr Sand. 'The Red Apprentice disappeared some weeks ago. We think he was kidnapped by Pigleg the pirate.'

The ordinary and apprentice Rainbow Wizards bowed to the King before taking their seats on the opposite side of the chamber. Louis marvelled at the magnificent sight of all the wizards lined up in rows as seven more gongs rang out.

Gong! Gong! Gong! Gong! Gong! Gong! Gong!

Seven more robed wizards entered the Prism Chamber.

'Chief Rainbow Wizards,' whispered Mr Sand.

Louis looked at the seven wizards. Their robes were long and flowing too, but much more magnificent, with gold braid all around the edges and decorations in silver and bronze. Unlike the other wizards, they had big hoods draped over their heads, so that their faces were almost completely obscured. From the side, Louis could just see the tips of their noses.

Reddadom, the Red Wizard, led the wizards in and stood in front of the red chair at the red segment of the table. Then the other wizards, Oranclees, Yellowell, Grenlapp, Bluwanuth, Indigon and Violothan, each stood in front of their respective coloured chair.

The King spoke in a commanding voice.

'Let the Seven Rays of The One Light unite.'

One gong sounded.

Gong!

FORTY-EIGHT

The White Light Ceremony

Louis watched as the Chief Rainbow Wizards sat down at the rainbow table.

With his left hand, each Rainbow Wizard brought from his robes a small crystal sphere and placed it in the hollow on the table in front of him. Louis noticed that each wizard had a sphere which matched the colour of his robes. The seven wizards kept their left hands on the spheres.

Then, all at the same time, the Chief Rainbow Wizards raised their wands with their right hands. Each wizard's wand was the same colour as his robes. The wizards all pointed their wands at the Prism of The One Light. They chanted in unison... *Let The One Light Shine!*

Louis watched with bated breath as each of the coloured crystals on the table began to glow under the palms of the wizards. Then something truly amazing happened. Seven rays of light, of each colour of the spectrum, beamed like lasers from the wands into Godolphin's Prism. In an instant, a beam of bright white light shot from the other side of the Prism, bouncing off the mirror and into the huge clear crystal sphere suspended above them. The Forcesphere's crystal generator began to glow incredibly brightly with white light.

Louis sat enthralled as the Seven Rays beamed into the Prism and out the other side as white light, making the generator glow brighter and brighter.

Then, suddenly, and without warning, Violothan rolled his violet-coloured crystal sphere from the table, drew from his robe a small, jet black stone, and rammed it into the empty hollow on the table; all the while keeping his violet wand pointed at the Prism.

'Death by *Skotos*! Long live the Lord of Darkness!' he cried, like a man possessed.

A black ray emanated from his wand.

'The Dark Beam!' exclaimed Mr Sand in horror.

'Run, Louis, RUN!'

FORTY-NINE

Darkness Day

Louis was rooted to his seat, paralysed by fear as he watched the events unfolding in the room. Everything was happening at once:

The six other Chief Wizards had no time to react to Violothan's treachery. Their hands seemed stuck to the crystal spheres in front of them, and their wands wobbled as the Dark Beam came back at each of them from the Prism. In an instant, the life-light was sucked from them. Their six shrivelled bodies slumped forward on to the table or fell sideways from the chairs.

The ordinary rainbow wizards reached in to their robes. A few managed to raise their wands to the traitor in their midst. But Violothan, still clutching *Skotos*, had taken them completely by surprise too. He was already sending the Dark Beam towards them.

'Death by *Skotos*! Die Rainbow Wizards!' he cried.

The Dark Beam fanned out, hitting all the ordinary wizards and the apprentices at the same time. They all fell to the ground, their skins shrivelled like raisins by the life-draining power of *Skotos* and the Dark Beam.

Violothan turned his attention to the Prism, mirror, and crystal generator. Aiming the Dark Beam at each in turn, he shouted at the top of his voice.

'Destroy by *Skotos*!'

The Prism, mirror, and generator cracked, shattered, and exploded as they were struck by the Dark Beam. A huge, black mushroom-shaped cloud rose into the air through the open dome.

'That blasted bubble will thwart us no more!' yelled Violothan. 'Now the invasion can go ahead, Young Master.'

He was looking straight across the room at Prince Manaccan.

'What treachery is this!?' shouted the King, staring aghast at his nephew.

'Mine!' shouted Prince Manaccan, as he lunged across the Queen and plunged a dagger into his uncle's heart.

'I WILL BE KING!'

'Nohhhhh!' screamed the Queen, but her plea was silenced by a blow from the hilt of Manaccan's dagger.

'The King is dead, long live King Manaccan!' shouted Violothan.

'Over my dead body,' exclaimed Princess Kea, as she grabbed her father's sword and aimed its point at Prince Manaccan's chest.

He moved deftly to the side as she thrust the weapon forward. The sword stuck in Manaccan's shoulder. He grimaced with the pain, but managed an ironic laugh.

'Ha, my pretty cousin shows plenty of spirit as usual. You'll pay for that later!' With that, he knocked the Princess to the ground with his fist, where she lay motionless on the cold stone floor.

'Come on, Lizard, we've got to raise the alarm,' shouted Professor Mullion. He was no warrior, but he *was* a good man. He ran for the door to warn others about the treachery afoot in the Prism Chamber. Dr Lizard leapt up and began running with him towards the door.

Then the doctor put out his foot and tripped the professor to the ground.

'Not so fast Mullion... we're going to need you.'

* * *

Louis had been in shock, watching the events unfolding as if they were in slow motion. He now realised that Mr Sand was pushing him.

'You must run. You must run.'

Louis suddenly came to his senses. He ran.

Manaccan threw his dagger at the running prince.

As the weapon span through the air, Mr Sand dived in front of his young pupil.

Louis was knocked to the ground as Mr Sand fell on him.

Laying on the floor, he heard his teacher groaning in pain.

Louis rolled out from under Mr Sand's body.

The dagger was sticking out of his teacher's back.

'Nohhhhhh,' wailed Louis.

But, before he had time to worry further about Mr Sand, out of the corner of his eye, Louis saw that his scream had attracted Violothan's attention. The Violet Wizard raised his wand once more and pointed it at the trembling young Prince.

Bang! Suddenly, Violothan was distracted by the opening of the doors.

The four guards had burst in, with pistols drawn, intent on discovering the reason for the commotion they had heard from outside.

Violothan aimed the Dark Beam from his wand at the soldiers as they entered.

'Death by *Skotos*! Die, guards!'

All four men shrivelled and fell in an instant.

This distraction had given Louis just enough time to act.

He pulled out his catapult, reached for an orange cataball, loaded, and fired at the rainbow table.

BOOM! The explosion threw Manaccan, Violothan and

Lizard from their feet.

Wood, stone, and metal flew in all directions.

Louis was covered in dust and rubble and splinters of wood.

Mr Sand moaned again. He motioned for Louis to come closer. The old man could hardly speak.

'I need to tell you the password to get back to your home through the Crystal Pool.'

Louis leaned forward. Mr Sand whispered in his ear.

'Go now, while you have the chance. Use what you have learned to find and rescue your sister. You'll need this Golden Key, to enter the Golden Cavern.

'And please... try to find the Red Wizard's apprentice; he may be on *The Revenger* too. All the other Rainbow Wizards have fallen this dark day. That boy is the last hope for Kernowland and Erthwurld.

'Good luck, Prince Louis. May The One Light be with you.'

Louis sobbed as Mr Sand's eyes closed and his body went limp.

* * *

The mushroom cloud rose high into the sky and spread out above Truro. The Prism Chamber was clouded by dust and covered in darkness.

The traitors were stirring from the effects of the cataball blast.

Louis knew this would be his very last chance to run. He ran.

FIFTY

Hughey The Huer

It was Midsummer's Morning.

Hughey the huer had slept in his hut and had just woken up.

His job was to look out for shoals of fish. When he saw the right size shoal, he would give a special signal to the fishermen that they should go out in their boats, by blowing his big horn three times.

The huer yawned and stretched. He then padded sleepily to the window and looked out over Towan Blystra bay.

At first he could not believe his eyes. He rubbed them to make sure. But he had seen it. Or rather, them!

Ramdragons! All flying in fan formation. All breathing fire.

All heading directly towards Kernowland.

Hughey grabbed up his horn, ran outside, and blew with all his might.

Horrrrrrrrnnnnnn! Horrrrrrrrnnnnnn! Horrrrrrrrnnnnnn!

He kept on blowing.

Horrrrrrrrnnnnnn! Horrrrrrrrnnnnnn! Horrrrrrrrnnnnnn!

He had to warn everyone.

The ramdragons flew overhead at low altitude.

Their sheer size and number blotted out the sun.

The terrified huer could hear their leathery wings flapping.

Nine of the trailing ramdragons were carrying cages.

Hughey could just make out what was in them.

'TROGS!'

FIFTY-ONE

The Snarebolas

After a very long journey, Dribble, Clevercloggs, and Heavyfeather had Kernow Castle in sight at last.

'Not long now,' said the old gnome, 'as they walked wearily along the road. Suddenly, Dribble's heart began pounding as he heard the faint sound of an engine.

Whrrrrrrrrrrrrrrrrrrrrrrrrrr.

'Wendron's Skycycle!' exclaimed Clevercloggs.

Moments later, out of the clouds, came Wendron and Drym on the flying contraption. They were in a steep dive.

Drym aimed a stunstone.

It scored a direct hit on Heavyfeather's head. The big swan fell sideways, with Clevercloggs still on his back, trapping the leg of the gnome underneath him.

'HAHAHAA! We've got them now!' shrieked Wendron in triumph.

Dribble ran over to Clevercloggs and tried to pull him out from under the swan using his teeth.

The Skycycle was coming in for a second dive.

Drym aimed a second stunstone.

This time Wendron was going so fast that Drym slipped before he could release his missile.

The Skycycle pulled up again rising steeply into the air.

Splutt! Splutt! Splutt!

The steep dive and climb had strained the Skycycle beyond its limits, and there was now a sputtering, spluttering sound coming from the exhaust.

The craft came spiralling down towards the ground,

completely out of control.

Wendron crash-landed in a ploughed field.

Drym was first out, waving Spikey wildly as he came striding forwards.

Wendron followed not far behind, thrashing Whackit up and down and cackling manically.

'It's the diary they're after,' said Clevercloggs. 'Take it to the castle. I've written the decoding in there.'

Dribble was in a quandary as to what to do, but the wise old gnome was insistent.

'Go now!' he shouted. 'For Kernowland and the children.'

Dribble was still unsure about leaving his friend.

But Drym and Wendron were nearly upon them.

'GO NOW!' shouted Clevercloggs again, much louder this time.

Finally, the little dog grabbed the diary in his teeth and started to run.

It was then that he saw a cloud of smoke in the shape of a mushroom, billowing out all over Truro City, cloaking it in darkness.

The terrible sight stopped him in his tracks.

Scrrrrrrrrrrrrrrrrrrrrrrrr.

A moment later, Dribble heard another sound. It was a bit like the Skycycle, but not as loud.

Turning back to look in the direction of the sound, Dribble saw Warleggan shooting along in the air about ten feet off the ground.

The warlock sped over the heads of Drym and Wendron, his long Warcoat flapping in his wake as he swirled the snarebolas above his head with one hand, whilst using the other to guide the Skyscooter.

Dribble put his nose down and started to run again... but he was no match for the speed of the Skyscooter.

Shhh. Shhh. Shhh.

The little dog heard the snarebolas whirling through the air towards him.

He felt it wrap around his back legs; around and around until he was brought to the ground with a crunch.

Warleggan flew over Dribble, leaving a trail of toxic exhaust smoke in his wake.

Dribble couldn't move. He began to tremble and whimper as he saw Drym stomping towards him.

The little dust dog's life-long tormentor was snarling and waving Spikey wildly and shouting at the top of his voice.

'THAT DROOLING DOG!

'HE'S FOR IT NOW, SPIKEY!

'OH YES HE IS!'

FIFTY-TWO

Twysta!

Earlier in the day, Captain Pigleg had avoided conflict with the Emperor's ships by taking evasive action. It was getting hotter and hotter as the pirates sailed further and further south.

Tizzie, Jack, Masai, and Hans had been given deck scrubbing duty. The delicate little girl, unused to hard physical labour, sweltered under the burning sun as she pushed the scrubbing brush backwards and forwards.

'Twysta ahoy!' cried Squint.

Tizzie and Jack stood up and looked over the water.

Out to sea, in the distance, a twirling tornado created a whirlpool and huge circular ripple-waves as it moved at high speed across the water.

The whirling wind was heading straight for the ship.

It was travelling at incredible speed.

'Make ready for Twysta!' shouted Pigleg.

All the pirates scurried around and tied things down as best they could. Those in the rigging hurriedly descended to the deck as the sails flapped and flailed in the gale force power of the oncoming wind.

As it approached, Twysta suddenly seemed to increase its speed and force.

'Quickly, lie down and hold on tight to something. Anything!' shouted Jack to the others.

All tried to do as instructed.

But Tizzie was too slow.

Twysta whirled into the ship and swept her off her feet.

As she was carried up into the air, she gashed her leg on a splintered edge of the port rail.

Blood poured from the gash and down over her foot.

'Slave overboard!' shouted Purgy. 'And there's blood!'

'Get my bait back on this ship!' barked Pigleg, as the wind rocked *The Revenger* violently from side to side.

The whirling storm was gone as quickly as it had come.

Tizzie thrashed about in the water, bobbing up and down with her head going under every few seconds. The waves left in Twysta's wake made the sea choppy. She couldn't help but gulp in seawater as she struggled to keep her head above the surface.

As Tizzie bobbed up for the fourth time, she heard an ominous sound.

It was a thrashing, threshing, bubbling, burbling sound in the near-distance.

The sound got louder and louder.

She saw the water foaming and frothing in front of her. A thousand small, black, frenzying dorsal fins protruded above the foam and froth. They looked about two hundred swimstrokes away.

Tizzie heard Squint's shout, as he pointed to the mass of froth and fins coming straight for her at incredible speed.

'PIRANHASHARKS!'

FIFTY-THREE

Alone

Louis ran past the four slain guards.

He ran down the stone spiral staircase.

He ran through the doors of the Map Room.

He ran on to the Mosaic Map.

He opened the locktile and, with trembling fingers, inserted the Golden Key.

He pulled open the mapdoor and started down the steps, taking care to shut the door above him.

He made his way down the twelve steps and hugged the wall of the dark passageway until he felt, with his outstretched foot, the first of the stone stairs that would lead him spiralling down to the Golden Cavern.

He went down the steps as quickly as he could in the darkness.

After what seemed like an endless spiral of stairs, he saw the flickering lights of the permacandles up ahead.

Made it, he thought, as he grabbed up *Zoomer* and threw its case strap over his shoulder.

But what next?

What did Mr Sand say was a good plan?

Oh, yes. Get to Nwotegroeg in Sandland through the Crystal Door.

Wait for Tizzie to arrive.

Rescue her.

And, if you can, find the Red Wizard's apprentice.

Then he had another thought.

I don't know if I can do all that; I'm only seven and three-quarters.

Nevertheless, the brave young boy he knew he had to try.

He put his hand on the hard Crystal Door and said out loud: 'Nwotegroeg, Aibmag, Sandland, Acirfa.'

The hard rock began to soften beneath his palm.

Summoning all his courage, the terrified young boy stepped into the soft green crystal.

For the first time in his life, little Louis felt truly alone.

FIFTY-FOUR

Now Is The Hour

Year Two at Towan Blystra Primary School had just finished Registration.

'Please, Miss Perfect,' said Tommy Tremar, raising his hand, 'can I go to the toilet, please.'

'Yes, Tommy, but be quick. The first lesson today is Storytime.'

'Yehhhsss!' cheered all the children at once; they loved Storytime.

'Quiet down now,' said Miss Perfect.

Tommy got up from his seat.

As he did so, he happened to glance out of the window.

There, in the sky, was a huge ball of fire, heading straight for the school.

'L... Look, M... Miss Perfect...' he murmured, pointing a trembling finger.

Reacting with lightning speed, and with only the protection of the children in her mind, Miss Perfect stood up and shouted to her class as she moved swiftly down the central aisle.

'Quickly children, under your desks... NOW!'

All the children dived for cover under their desks, with Miss Perfect giving some a helpful push on their way.

There was a roaring sound as the blazeball approached.

Seconds later, the flaming bomb landed in the playground.

A huge blast ripped through the school buildings.

Tommy heard the window-glass shatter. Sharp, jagged splinters flew in all directions around the classroom.

A few moments later, Tommy was the first to emerge

from below his desk.

Some of the children were screaming. Others had their hands over their ears.

Tommy saw his friend, Wendy Rock, bending over the prostrate form of the teacher.

'Miss Perfect, wake up, wake up,' he heard her say.

Tommy was only six, and he wasn't quite sure what to do.

It was at that moment that Joharvy Par put his head in the room. Joh was ten years old and much bigger than Tommy and his friends.

'Everyone! Out of school now,' he shouted.

'But remember, walk don't run!'

As the flames and smoke spread rapidly around them, Tommy led the way out of the classroom.

Outside, apart from some nasty cuts and bruises, all his friends seemed to have survived the blast without serious injury.

Tommy watched as Joh Par and two of his friends dragged Miss Perfect's lifeless form out into the playground.

The Ramraiders on their ramdragons were dropping thousands of propaganda leaflets as well as blazebombs.

A leaflet floated down beside Tommy.

At that moment, there was another huge explosion as a second blazebomb scored a direct hit on the Assembly Hall.

Tommy grabbed up the leaflet and dived for cover.

His hands trembled as he read the words:

> Now is the hour,
> Of Darkness Day.
> Evile, your Emperor,
> Is on his way.
> Submit, to serve,
> And you may survive.
> Resist, and by midnight,
> YOU WON'T BE ALIVE!

- NEXT -

After reading, *Darkness Day*, the second book in the Kernowland series, you may want certain questions answered:

What will Louis find beyond the Crystal Door?

Will Tizzie be de-fleshed by the piranhasharks?

How can Dribble possibly escape from Drym and Spikey?

What will Wendron and Warleggan do to Clevercloggs?

Will Misty suffocate or become an ice-dessert for Meow?

Will Plumper and the other gnomes be roasted alive on Old Oaky?

Are the King, Queen, and Mr Sand all dead?

What are Manaccan's plans for Princess Kea?

Why do the traitors need Professor Mullion?

Will Miss Perfect wake up?

Who will the trogs eat first?

Will Kernowland be able to resist the invasion?

If so, you may get some answers by reading Book 3, the next title in the exciting Kernowland series:

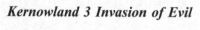

Kernowland 3 Invasion of Evil

Visit our websites for up-to-date information about new titles, publication dates, and popular school visits by the author

www.kernowland.com
www.erthwurld.com